THE WASHING AWAY OF WRONGS

Also by M Clement Hall

Non-Fiction
The Locomotor System—Functional Anatomy
The Locomotor System—Functional Histology
Architecture of Bone
Luschka's Joint
Lessons in Histology
Palestine—The Price of Freedom
IME—The Word Book
Independent Medical Examinations
The Fibromyalgia Controversy
Intifada

Memoir
Viet Nam 1963
Viet Nam 1964-1966
Vale Viet Nam

Fiction
Trauma Surgeon
The Spare Parts Box
Martin's Absolution
Martin in Byzantium
Diamonds in West Africa
Farmer George
The George Inn

THE WASHING AWAY OF WRONGS

by
Song Ci (1186-1249)

Translated from the Chinese by
Herbert A. Giles (1845-1935)
Professor of Chinese, Cambridge University

Edited by
M Clement Hall

Published 2010 by Lulu
The Washing Away of Wrongs

ISBN 978-0-557-41927-2

THE HSI YUAN LU
or
THE WASHING AWAY OF WRONGS
INSTRUCTIONS TO CORONERS
Original Preface

The Hsi Yüan Lu dates from the reign Shun Yu [A.D 1241-1253] of the after Sung dynasty, and was compiled by a Commissioner of Justice named Sung Tz'u from the *I Yü Chi* by Ho Ning, Duke of Lu under the Chin dynasty and his son Meng, aide-de-camp to the Heir Apparent under the first Sung dynasty; also from the *Nei Shu Lu* by an unknown author of the Sung dynasty, and from various other books. Being subjected for many generations to practical tests by the officers of the Board of Punishments, it became daily more perfect and more exact.

The work now published by the Board was compiled from the *P'ing Yüan Lu* by an unknown author of the after Sung dynasty, from the *Wu Yüan Lu* by Wang Yü of the Yüan dynasty, and the *Hsi Yüan Lu Chien Shih* by Wang K'en-t'ang of the Ming dynasty, and is strictly adhered to by all engaged in the investigation of criminal cases. Yet although in general use among officials, good editions are rarely to be met with in booksellers' shops. A collection of corroborative cases have lately been supplied by Wang Yu-huai of Wu-lin, an additional commentary by Sub-Prefect Yüan Ch'i-hsin of Kueichi, and coloured punctuation by Prefect Chang Hsi-fan of Yüan-ho, making a thoroughly intelligible and complete work. As, however, the blocks are unfortunately kept in Kuangsi, copies are seldom seen in the South (Kuangtung); wherefore, Chung Hsiao-t'ing, a secretary of the Privy Council, from Chiang-tu, desirous of rendering it widely known, has, after careful revision, brought out a new edition.

I, the writer of this Preface, finding that both the summary and supplement of Book V in the original work were comprised in the above-mentioned corroborative cases and additional supplement; also, that the appendices *Pao Chien P'ien* and *Shih Hsiang Pi Lu* were a lot of doggerel rhymes in a vulgar style and of no practical value for reference, had just expunged them one and all, when I happened to come across, on the table of Hsü Shih-hua of Hai-chow, an Imperial Professor, a work entitled *Tso Li Yao Yen* or "Important Counsels to Government Officers," by a Fukien magistrate Yeh Yü-p'ing, commented upon and explained by Chu Hsing-chai of Yün-chien, a head Censor, to which was added a series of twelve additional articles from his own "limited experience." The language being terse and perspicuous, easy to understand and easy to act up to, and of special value to public servants, I substituted it for what I had just expunged, as an appendix to the Hsi Yüan Lu: that all officials purchasing copies might not only derive benefit as regards the investigation of cases, but, further, have their attention called to the fundamental principle of physical and moral government. Thus, an honourable discharge of their duties manifesting itself among officials and a system of virtue and decorous behaviour growing up among the people, the dead would be without wrongs and the living in the enjoyment of happiness, a consummation unceasingly hoped for by Yeh and Chu, and devoutedly wished by Judge Sung!

Done at Huai-pei, in the 9th moon of the 23rd year of the reign Tao Kuang (1843),
by T'ung Lien, a Sub-Prefect of the Salt Gabelle.

Translator's Preface

The office and functions of coroner, in the modern sense of the term, were known to the Chinese many centuries before "Crowner's Quest Law" was quoted in Hamlet.

It was while stationed at Ningpo, in 1873, that I first heard of the Hsi-yüan-lu. I found that a copy of this work, here translated, was always carried to the scene of an inquest by the high territorial official on whom the duties of coroner devolved. I also found that inquests were held on the living, when dangerously wounded, as well as on the dead. In the latter case, to move or disturb in any way a corpse, before the coroner had seen and examined it, would lead to the most serious consequences for such reckless interference.

I became sufficiently interested in this phase of Chinese civilization to proceed to a careful study of the text of the Hsi-yüan-lu, and thence to translation, for which I was repaid by the possession of some acquaintance with the system of medical jurisprudence in ancient China.

Herbert A. Giles
Cambridge, 1923

Editor's Preface

This ancient book is well known, but to a very small group of people. The author seems to have been a combination of today's European Examining Magistrate, and the American Medical Examiner.

Dr Giles translates his words to "Coroner" which to an Englishman of his generation may have seemed appropriate, and certainly the early coroner was the King's man whose function it was to investigate the untoward incidents of his Shire.

Song Ci had more skills than a mere investigator and his observations one feels are based on a great deal of experience. His remedies probably were also based on experience, though he had more confidence in them than most doctors would have today, either in his or in their own.

My purpose in preparing the book for publication, is to show how very old is "Forensics" as a science, and to give ourselves reason to look back and to consider the powers built on observation and experience.

I have pleasure in making Song Ci's book available to a wider readership than academia.

MCH
Guelph, Canada
2010

TABLE OF CONTENTS
BOOK ONE

BOOK ONE
CHAPTER ONE
General Remarks on Inquests

There is nothing more important than human life; there is no punishment greater than death. A murderer gives life for life: the law shows no mercy. But to obviate any regrets which might be occasioned by a wrong infliction of such punishment, the validity of a confession (in order to prevent rich criminals from procuring substitutes) and the sentence passed are made to depend on a satisfactory examination of the wounds. If these are of a bona-fide nature and the confession of the accused tallies therewith, then life may be given for life, that those who know the laws may fear them, that crime may become less frequent among the people, and due weight be attached to the sanctity of human existence. If an inquest is not properly conducted, the wrong of the murdered man is not redressed, new wrongs are raised up amongst the living, other lives sacrificed, and both sides roused to vengeance of which no man can foresee the end.

In important cases, where death has not already ensued, all will depend on the energy of the coroner in proceeding instantly to personal examination of the victim noting down the wounds, their position and severity, and fixing the death-limit, (period of responsibility) in the hope that medical skill may effect a cure; so that in case of re-examination after death with a view to obtain a [different] verdict, the unpleasantness of dissection may be avoided.

Where death has already resulted from the wounds there is still greater need for promptitude ere decomposition sets in, and while as yet it is easy to note the severity and size of each wound. For while you are delaying the body is beginning to decompose though to guard against the infliction of false, or the tampering with real wounds is a principle of the highest importance. No, the coroner and his assistants should

11

hasten to the spot with all speed, that the guilty parties may have no time to concoct schemes for evading the consequences of their crime.

If death has just taken place, first examine the top of the head, and the back, the ears, the nostrils, the throat, etc., and all places where anything might be inserted, on the chance of finding a sharp-pointed instrument of some kind or other. If nothing is found, proceed to examine the body in the regular way.

Should it be a case where examination of the bones is necessary, first carefully interrogate the relatives of the deceased, neighbours, and the accused, bidding them state clearly who struck whom with what weapon, and in what part of the body, the deposition of each being taken down in writing. Then, with your assistants, petitioner, and accused, proceed to the spot where the body lies, and examine it as the law directs. Mark what wounds are on vital spots, whether on the trunk or extremities, whether skin or flesh wounds, whether penetrating to the bone, their colour, size and shape; whether inflicted by the hand or foot, or by some weapon; their severity and appearance, whether recent or old. All this must be carefully elucidated and the prescribed form filled up with your own hand, not by the assistants. Do not, deterred by the smell of the corpse, sit at a distance, your view intercepted by the smoke of fumigation, letting the assistants call out the wounds and enter them on the form, perhaps garbling what is of importance and giving prominence to what is not, adding or subtracting as they see fit. Moreover, deaths from self-strangulation, throat-cutting, taking poison, burning, drowning, and the like, produce very different results, and only the most minute investigation of every little detail will ensure a complete and reliable verdict. If this be neglected, the assistants will intrigue and make light of the whole affair; the culprit will devise some means for escaping punishment, the relatives of the deceased will appeal against your decision,

12

mischief-makers and bad characters will seize the opportunity, and the end of it all will be that your verdict will be discredited, another Coroner deputed, and dissection of the corpse be a matter of necessity, an outrage on the dead, an inconvenience to the living. These are the evils attendant on a dilatory or perfunctory discharge of your duties.

In all cases where the circumstances are unusually suspicious, extra care must be taken to make the fullest inquiries. For instance, where death has taken place within the death-limit from wounds the cicatrices of which are not distinct, if there be any appearance of illness, it should be asked whether deceased was in the habit of employing doctors, quacks, or the like. Many die from disease, but you are not likely to find this out if you do not ask. It will not, however, do to trust to the testimony of a single person, or to be anything but cautious in employing others to make inquiries lest you defeat your own purpose.

In all cases of death where the relatives of the deceased, not having been absent, have not petitioned till more than a year has elapsed, or where it is not the relatives who file petition but some outsider, or where the more important facts are relegated from the body of the petition to the accompanying statement of circumstances in detail; in all such instances no hasty measures should be taken.

In all cases where requests are preferred, even by near relatives, that examination may be dispensed with; it will be necessary to satisfy yourself that there actually is a corpse (in order to prevent false accusations with the object of extorting money, followed up, when the money has been paid, by petitions for "no examination") at the place mentioned before granting the petition.

Care must be taken that neither your own assistants, nor any person mixed up in the case, give notice beforehand to the four next-door neighbours and assist them in absconding; arresting only more distant neighbours, old men, women and children, thereby acting up to the letter of their duty in producing some one. Also that the accused conceal no important witness or bona-fide evidence for his own ends, and that he produce no witnesses, either friends, dependants, or tenants and the like, whose evidence at the inquest is false.

Any delay in securing the weapon which caused death will be taken advantage of by the accused's family for concealing the same. Your case would be thus rendered incomplete, and disastrous consequences would ensue. The weapon should be secured at once for future comparison with the wounds as to length and breadth, in order to complete the case.

At all inquests the first thing to be done is to cause the body to be identified by relatives and neighbours. If, however, it is in too advanced a stage of decomposition, they must be examined as to the colour and shape of the clothes deceased had on, if there were any marks on them, and also what scars or marks he might have had on his body. Their answers must be taken down in writing and signed before the examination begins.

The report on an inquest should show where and in what position the body was found, as also each article of clothing it had on; whether there were any tattoo marks, traces of acupuncture or cauterization; whether any limbs were found broken before death; whether hump-backed, having one leg shorter than the other, or bald; the colour of any marks on the body; the presence of tumours, swelled legs, and such like complaints. All these should be carefully noted in case of a further examination being held, or, where deceased's name was unknown, the body being claimed hereafter by relatives, in which case their statements could be put to the test. When criminals die in prison, those points must be attended to with more than usual minuteness.

The object of re-examinations is not to verify a previous verdict, but to guard against any injustice being done.

14

If, therefore, any Coroner thus appointed, losing sight of the importance of human life, allow the least shadow of a wrong to remain unredressed, either from fear of offending the officer who presided at the previous examination, or from unwillingness to release the accused who may happen to be wealthy, from anxiety to suit the report to the wishes of superior officers, or from an endeavour to make the present resemble past cases, and so get quit of his duty as soon as possible, his crime will be greater in degree than that of the Coroner who held the first inquest. Rather let every Coroner deputed proceed with caution and justice to make the most careful investigation possible; for the object in examining a corpse is to arrive at the unvarnished truth, and where it is a case of a wounded man whose life is trembling in the balance, the slightest private bias should not be thrown into the scale.

In cases of severe wounds on vital spots where death was instantaneous or resulted within three days, and where petitioner and witnesses can swear to the weapon and the part struck, it will only be necessary to examine such wound, thus sparing the dead all superfluous handling, and preventing injustice being done to the living. For men, in their passage from youth to manhood, either by falling down and striking against something, or being thumped and rubbed for pains, from the accidental breaking of a boil, carrying heavy weights, or knocking against hard things, cause their blood to be arrested in its course. Where the wounds are slight and of recent date, the bone will be of a red colour, which will pass away in time. Where the wounds are old and severe, the bone will be dark blue in colour, and will remain so to the last. It frequently happens that petitioner and witnesses mention a particular blow behind the ear as the cause of death, whereas on examination the body is found to be covered with wounds, and the higher authorities cancel the inquest as inaccurate. An officer who, in adding circumstances to make his report tally, were to mention wounds on both sides of exactly the same size

15

and colour, would be met, if death resulted from blows, by the question: "Had the accused a similar weapon in each hand, and was there no difference in the force of each blow dealt ? " Sometimes after a drunken brawl at night it will be confidently asserted that such a man struck in such a part. Now when the combatants themselves do not know where or remember how many blows each struck, is it likely that witnesses could? Generally speaking, where several people are engaged in a melee, in adjudging punishment you should look to the origin of the fray; in examining wounds, the important point is to ascertain their exact positions. Do not, however, adhere too closely to rules, as thereby injustice may be done; neither act with indecision or you will assuredly commit some blunder.

Where several persons strike blows it is difficult to determine which was the fatal blow. If on the body of the deceased there are two mortal wounds, both inflicted by the same man, he alone is responsible. If they were inflicted by different persons, one only pays the penalty of death, the most severe being held to be the mortal wound.

Where there are several wounds, fix on one as the mortal wound.

It is common for wounds to be set down by the accused as self-inflicted by deceased knocking in various ways against things, to the great hindrance of a proper elucidation of facts and settlement of the case. Knocking against things at rest is called *k'o*; running up against things in motion is called *chuang*. Such wounds would be confined to the front of the body, the forehead, etc., and being self-inflicted would not be severe; at any rate, not severe enough to cause death. Wounding oneself behind by running backwards against anything is quite out of the question. Where deceased has been knocked down and has wounds on the back of his head, back, or ribs, in as much as he may have been violently thrown down by the accused and have died from the effects of the fall, it will be necessary to observe carefully whether the body was lying

16

on its back or its belly, and to note the severity of the wounds. These must not be hastily entered as wounds received by knocking against things, etc., or a miscarriage of justice will be the result.

CHAPTER TWO
General Remarks on Examining Wounds
And Fixing the Death-limit

Murders are rarely the result of premeditation, but can be traced in the majority of cases, to a brawl. The statute which treats of wounding in a brawl attaches great weight to the death-limit, which means that the wounded man be handed over to the accused to be taken care of and provided with medical aid, and that a limit of time be fixed, on the expiration of which punishment be awarded according to circumstances. Now the relatives of a wounded man, unless their ties be of the closest, generally desire his death that they may extort money from his slayer; but the accused wishes him to live that he himself may escape death, and therefore leaves no means untried to restore him to health. This institution of the death-limit is a merciful endeavour to save the lives of both.

Cases of battery should always be reported by the ti-pao or head man before anyone else, and any neglect on his part should be punished severely. Where death has ensued, near relatives of the deceased, such as father, brother, uncle, sister, wife, or child, who saw the corpse undressed on the day the wounds were inflicted, should be interrogated as to the age of the deceased, the month, day, and hour, at which the wounds were received, the weapon used, and the part struck. Their replies will give you, for instance, an oblique wound in such and such a spot, of such and such a length, or the circumference and diameter of any round wounds there may be, whether livid or red, swollen or not swollen, whether or not the skin or bone was broken, and what witnesses there were, all of which must be entered in due form in the accusation. Where death has not ensued, summon and examine the head man, and if the wounds are really grave, do not let the sufferer be brought up for inspection lest death might result from the exposure of his wounds, but go at once to the place yourself, on

18

horseback or in a sedan, with a few attendants only, and proceed to examination, noting the wounds and fixing a death-limit. Accused should also be instructed to take the wounded man to his own home and see that he is properly treated. Meanwhile the case stands over. On the day death takes place, and formal application is made for an inquest, the evidence, etc., taken at the previous examination should be gone through and the wounds identified; all mortal wounds being carefully re-examined if there is the slightest cause for suspicion. Care in the early stages may be the saving of the lives of many who are mixed up in the case. If it is a trumped-up affair, make it clear that it is so, to warn people from like attempts in future. If it is bona-fide, take down the evidence and confession at once, to prevent any advances being improperly made towards you. See that your assistants, petitioner, accused, and the witnesses are all present, and make them sign the necessary declarations to that effect. Then, in summing up and awarding punishment, be still more careful that every point has been brought out clearly, and that there are no doubts in your own mind; for by these means, not only will justice be done to the living and to the dead, but you will prevent the cancelling of your inquest, long months and years of delay, and the implication of many persons. Where the petitioner has failed to report a case [of wounding] and to apply for the fixing of the death-limit, petitioning only when death has taken place, except in cases where it was instantaneous or within three days, in which instances the inquest may proceed as usual. It will be necessary to be very much on one's guard against counterfeit wounds. If, before reporting a case to the proper authorities, the opportunity is seized for carrying the corpse to the door [of the accused's house] seizing on his goods and wounding people, this second case must be settled as well as the first and a death-limit fixed according to circumstances. Should a death-limit be partly in one month and partly in another, you must observe whether the first is a long or a short month: there must be no

19

carelessness about the limit of life and death. In a word, the examination of a body should be performed speedily and without making light of it; the examination of bones should be performed carefully, and without needlessly breaking them. If the report of an inquest is rejected by the higher authorities because confused in detail of the circumstances, investigate the circumstances only; if they complain of discrepancies as regards the wounds, then examine the wounds; but do not take any unnecessary steps.

There are vital spots and mortal wounds. The top of the head, behind the ear, the throat, the pit of the stomach, etc., belong to the former class; death soon takes place. Other ordinarily vital spots are the back of the head, the forehead, the chest, etc. Mortal wounds are where the flesh is livid, the skin broken, there is a deep gash, bones broken, brains coming out, blood flowing, etc. Where a mortal wound is given on a vital spot of the kind first mentioned, death will result in three days; on an ordinarily vital spot, in ten days. If a slight wound has been given on a vital spot, or a severe wound on a non-vital spot, though death ensue within the limit, yet other circumstances should be taken into consideration and allowed to influence your verdict. This applies still more forcibly if death occurs after the death-limit.

The death-limit is the most important point of all. Immediately on a case being reported, make a personal examination of the wounds and fix the limit accordingly. If death ensues from improper medical treatment, make a calculation of the time, so as to determine whether within or without the limit. Also take a note of the time at which the wounds were received, that your case may be clear and complete.

CHAPTER THREE
Form for Entering Wounds

Sixteen vital spots are enumerated on the front of the body, and six on the back; thirty-six non-vital spots on the front, and twenty on the back. These are supposed to be shown in the accompanying diagrams (two outlines of body with Chinese characters).

CHAPTER FOUR
Examination of the Body

Where a corpse has to be examined prepare for use plenty of onions, red pepper, salt, and white prunes, also grains and vinegar, in case the wounds are indistinct or invisible. Take besides an earthenware basin, with implements for breaking, powdering, etc.

Do not be deterred by the smell and above all do not let the assistants intercept your view of any part of the body, as this would be a very serious hindrance.

Only on the discovery of a mortal wound can you insist on the relatives of deceased and the accused being present at the proceedings. On no account allow them to come too near for fear of damaging the body.

Begin to examine from the head downwards. Measure the length of the hair, noting if any has been pulled out or cut off. Look under the hair on the top of the head, and between that and the forehead, to see if there is any other cause of death, as a burn or a wound from a sharp-pointed weapon, etc. Examine the forehead and temples with the same view. Then the eyebrows, eyelids, and eyes. Note if the eyes are open or closed; if the latter, open them to see whether the pupils are perfect or not. Examine the cheek-bones to see if there are marks of a blow from a fist; the cheeks, whether tattooed or not, or whether such marks may have been obliterated. In the latter case, cut a slip of bamboo and tap the parts, when the

21

tattooing will reappear. Note if the ears have been bitten, grasped by the hand, cut or wounded; if the nostrils or any part of the nose have been pierced by any sharp instrument; and if the lips are opened or closed. Count the teeth, and observe if the tongue is protruding. Also examine the jaws. Into the throat insert a silver needle, and note if it is black when withdrawn. Examine the outside to see if it is swollen, and if there are any wounds which might have produced death. Feel with your hand the windpipe and gullet; examine the shoulders and arm-pits, for a severe wound in the last mentioned parts would cause death. Examine the arm, wrist, hand, and fingers, down to the quick of the nails. These are not vital spots in themselves, but were the bones broken, or the quick pierced, and not properly cured, death might result. Examine the chest, breasts, pit of the stomach, belly, ribs, etc., etc. These are nearly all vital spots. Examine the thighs, knees, shin-bones, ankles, instep, toes and toenails. The same remark applies here which referred above to the hand and fingers.

Examine the back of the head, noting if there are any marks of bruises on the "pillow-bone " from a fall, etc. Examine the hair, the nape of the neck, and behind the two ears. Examine the arm, elbow, and back of the hand as above. Examine between the shoulders to see if there are any marks of cauterization, the back generally, ribs, waist, etc. Note if the body bears marks of corporal punishment, and examine the inside of the knees, and the calves. Any scars on the ankle-bones, if both on the inside and outside, may be set down to torture; if on the outside only to a blow. Examine the heels, the sole of foot, under the toes, and the quick. These are not vital under ordinary circumstances.

Note the age of the man, and take his height and breadth across the shoulders; observe also the position of the wounds, and their nature, whether scrapes or bruises. Observe if they are of a dull livid red or black hue; and noting the size and extent of each, determine on the immediate cause of death.

Mark on what places there are scars of tattooing, cauterization, or boils, and note down whether recent or old, and whether or not there is any pus. Also, whether there are traces of the itch, sores, or other marks on the body, both natural and artificial. All such should be carefully written down, or marked as wanting.

In examining a body or skeleton where the wounds are not visible, spread grains and sprinkle some vinegar upon the corpse in the open oil-cloth umbrella and hold it between the sun and the parts you want to observe. The wounds will then appear. If the day is dark or rainy, use live charcoal [instead of the sun]. Suppose there is no result, then spread over the parts pounded white prunes with more grains and vinegar, and examine closely. If the result is still imperfect, then take the flesh only of the white prune, adding red pepper, onions, salt and grains, and mix it up into a cake. Make this very hot over a fire, and then, having first interposed a sheet of paper, lay it on the part. The wound will then appear.

Where death has resulted from blows, and the wounds have not been severe enough to break limbs, the flesh will adhere tightly to the bones, and if it cannot be washed away should be removed with the finger-nail, when the wounds will be visible [on the bone].

The human body is naturally red or brown, but after death it changes to a livid blue. Where no wounds are visible, only suspicious appearances, first sprinkle the corpse with water, then take the heart of an onion, smash it with a blow of the hand and lay it on the part, spreading over it a sheet of paper dipped in vinegar. Let it stay on a little while, then take it off and wash with water. The wound will thus appear. If there are several dark-coloured marks on the body, take some water and let it fall drop by drop on to them. If they are wounds, they will be hard and the water will remain without trickling away; if they are not, they will be soft and the water will run off.

23

In examining wounds, the finger must be used to press down any livid or red spot. If it is a wound it will be hard, and on raising the finger will be found of the same colour as before. If water is dropped on to it and the drops do not trickle away, it is undoubtedly a real wound. If it is a part which has changed colour it will turn white when the finger is pressed down on it, and water dropped on to it will not remain. Change of colour is caused by the blood in the bowels dispersing after death; not being able to congeal in any one place, it spreads over the whole surface. But where the blows were given before death, the blood congeals into a wound there where vitality ceases [i.e. at the spot struck]. Now the blood is dependent for its motion on vitality; if vitality stops, the blood stops also, hence the hardness.

There are certain parts such as the eyebrows, the windpipe and gullet, the ribs, etc., which are not marked as vital, but which may prove so if the wound happen to be very severe. This is an important point to remember at the time of examination. Any slight red marks on the back, thighs, calves, etc., are the result of the corpse lying on its back and the blood sinking to those parts: they are not connected with the cause of death.

Part Two
Examination of a Corpse Which Has Not Been Buried

Whether in a room, on the ground, or on a bed, or whether in the open air, behind or in front of a house, on a hill, in water, or the grass, you must first measure the exact position of a corpse with regard to surrounding objects. If in water, how far from the nearest hill or bank; also ask on whose ground, and the name of the place. If in a room, note in what part of it and if there is anything covering or spread underneath it. Then, and then only, should the body be removed for examination.

Begin by stripping off all the clothes etc., down to the shoes and stockings, taking
a note of each as well as anything else about the person. Then wash the body in warm
water before proceeding to examination. Grains and vinegar must not be used till this
is done.

Part Three
Examination after Temporary Burial

First see the grave, asking on whose land it is and the name of the place, and take the size and height of the mound. If the coffin has been placed temporarily in any one's house, take the measurements as before.

Next observe which way the head points. Suppose towards the east and the feet towards the west, then note how far each is from any particular spot, and the sides of the body in the same way. In the presence of all, remove the earth or bricks and observe what is spread underneath, whether the coffin is varnished or ornamented, and whether the mat, or whatever is under the corpse, has a border or not. Then remove the body to a convenient spot and proceed to examination.

CHAPTER FIVE
Washing and Preparing the Body

When the body has been removed to a convenient spot, first inspect it as it is. Then dash water over it. Next wash off every particle of dirt with soap, and throw more water over it, the corpse lying all the time on a door or a mat to keep it clean. This finished, grains and vinegar may be spread on as usual, the clothes of deceased laid over the body and saturated with hot vinegar, the whole being covered over with mats (to keep the steam in). In a little while, when the body has become soft, remove the coverings, wash off the grains and vinegar and proceed to examine. Do not trust too much to your assistants; if they only sprinkle spirit (without the grains) and vinegar the wounds will not appear.

Prepare plenty of grains and vinegar, also paper for putting under the body. The best kinds of the latter are *t'eng lien* and *pai ch'ao*. Bamboo paper is spoilt by vinegar and salt and may injure the body.

At the beginning of spring and during winter the vinegar and grains should be used very hot; in the middle of spring and towards the end of autumn they should be rather less so. In summer and autumn, if the grains and vinegar were at all hot, this, added to the heat of the weather, might cause injury to the skin. Late in autumn use them hot, and at a distance of from three to four feet on either side of the body light fires to stimulate their action.

In very cold weather, when the corpse is frozen hard and no amount of grains and vinegar, however hot, or clothes piled up, however thick, will relax its rigidity, dig a hole the length and breadth of the body and three feet in depth; lay in it a quantity of fuel and make a roaring fire. Then dash over it vinegar, which will create dense volumes of steam, in the middle of which place the body with all its dressings right in the hole, cover it with clothes and pour on more hot vinegar all

26

over it. At a distance of two or three feet from the hole on either side, light fires as before. When you think the heat has thoroughly penetrated, take away the fire and remove the body for examination.

At the end of winter and beginning of spring it will not be necessary to make a hole but merely to light fires on each side. This, however, must be left to the judgment of the Coroner.

CHAPTER SIX
First Examination of the Body

At a first examination, if it is a case where death resulted from blows, it will not do to report the corpse decomposed and therefore presenting no reliable features; but the scars must be carefully scrutinized and the causes of death ascertained. If from lapse of time decomposition has really taken place, the body may be reported as unfit to stand the necessary handling.

When the examination as to the presence or absence of wounds is over, leave the corpse on the mats in the exact spot where it was examined, cover it up and seal it all round with the lime seal, taking a note of the number of seals. Then hand over charge of the body to the head man of the place, and add his formal receipt to the records of the case as a precaution against any one tampering with or injuring the corpse.

Part Two
Further Examination

If the body is many days old, and the head and face have swollen up, the skin and hair come off, the lips turned back and the mouth open, and maggots have already made their appearance, then it is quite unfit for examination; and if the wounds were inflicted by a sharp or other weapon, or a blow of the hand or foot on a fleshy part where there is no bone, you may report that examination is impossible. But if the bone has been injured in any way, then the body must be washed and carefully inspected, and the cause of death ascertained. The plea used in the other case will not hold good.

The Coroner who thus re-examines should, on the completion of his task and if there is no dissentient voice, hand over the body to the nearest relatives. Where there are no near relatives, it may be entrusted to the head man who should be ordered to bury it and see that it comes to no harm. If there happen to be dissentient voices, then it must not be entrusted to any one, but dig a hole and in it lay the corpse with all its mats, etc.; cover it over with a door and pile up earth on the top. Then seal all round with the seal and take a note of the number of seals in case of there being a still further examination. The person left in charge must sign a formal declaration to that effect to be put with the records of the case.

At the end of the first or further examination the relatives of deceased or the head man should be instructed to take charge of the body but it should on no account be carried off to the Yamen, to their great inconvenience and for no particular object. The accused and the witnesses only should be arrested; the others can be summoned afterwards.

CHAPTER SEVEN
Decomposition Different at Different Seasons

In the spring months, when a body is two or three days old, the flesh of the nose, mouth, abdomen, sides and chest becomes slightly livid; after ten days a foul liquid issues from the mouth, nose and ears. The bodies of fat people swell and the skin separates from the flesh, which does not take place with the bodies of thin people or those who have been long ill, till more than half a month has elapsed

In the summer months, first the face and then the flesh on the belly, ribs, and chest changes colour in one or two days. In two or three days a foul liquid issues from the mouth and nose, and maggots appear. The whole body swells, the lips pout, the skin rots and separates from the flesh, blisters rise, and in four or five days the hair falls off.

In very hot weather, the injured parts of a body which has been prepared will be mostly covered with a white skin, but the uninjured parts will be dark coloured. The exact nature of the wounds it will be very difficult to distinguish, but if from a dread of the smell, etc., you fail to make a most searching examination, the result is sure to be unsatisfactory. Wherever there is the slightest suspicious appearance, the loose skin should be removed, and if there is a wound, there will be a hole-like appearance beneath it.

In very hot weather, supposing maggots appear at the temples or other places before appearing at either of the nine orifices, it will be because in that particular part there is a wound.

In the autumn months, two or three days produce the same effect as one or two in summer, and so on in proportion.

In the winter months, a corpse turns after four or five days to a yellowish purple. In half a month the flesh on the face, mouth, nose, etc., begins to decompose, but wrapping it in mats and placing it in a moist place will preserve it longer. Be careful to be guided by the seasons, not by the months.

In extremely hot weather, decomposition begins after one day, the body assuming a dark, dull, hue, and emitting a smell. In three or four days the flesh becomes rotten, maggots appear, a dark fluid issues from the mouth and nose, and the hair gradually falls off.

In spring and autumn, when the weather is mild, two or three days are equal to one in summer, and eight or nine to three or four. In very cold weather, five days are equal to one in summer, and half a month to three or four summer days.

CHAPTER EIGHT
To Distinguish Real and Counterfeit Wounds

In examining a body which is not yet decomposed, pay attention only to such parts as are red, swollen, cut or bruised, discriminating between mortal and non-mortal wounds. Such parts as are of a livid or purple colour need not occupy your time, as this hue is common to all bodies in a state of decomposition. Wounds on bones may be of various colours and shades, which are counterfeited in the following manner: red, by taking some genuine safflower, sapanwood, and black plums, and making them into an ointment, adding alum, and painting it on the bone, pouring over it boiling vinegar, when a red colour will be obtained of a darker or lighter shade exactly like that of a real wound; purple, by taking sapanwood and "earth's blood," and applying as before; dark blue or black, by taking green alum or nutgalls and mixing with vinegar into a thick liquid, regulating the proportions of each according as the shade required is light or dark. Though very deceptive, these counterfeits may be detected by the dullness of their colour, by their being apparent to the touch, and by the absence of the usual halo-like shading-off of colour all round. But everything depends on the energy displayed at the time of examination; there must be no carelessness.

Where blows have been given resulting in death, the injured parts will be surrounded by a purple or red halo. If, when death has already taken place, lighted bamboo strips have been used to burn a wound, which it is pretended was inflicted before death, the wound will present a scorched appearance, will be level with the surrounding flesh, and not hard to the touch. If the bark of the willow tree be used to make a wound, the flesh will be rotten and black, livid all round but without any swelling, and not hard to the touch. Counterfeit wounds are also made by lighting paper inside a cup and applying it to the flesh; such wounds resemble a blow from a fist, but all round there is a red scorched mark, the flesh inside is yellow, and although it swells, it does not get hard.

All wounds must be determined by the inflammation, which is the gradual diminishing of the wound, change of colour, from dark to lighter shades, and lessening of intensity. Also, near where the wound ends there should be a halo-like appearance, like rain seen from a distance, or like fleecy clouds, vague and indistinct, fresh-coloured and smooth-looking, a result which should proceed naturally from the infliction of the wound. This is the most important principle of all. If the red is by itself and purple by itself, of a dull colour and collected into one spot, there being moreover, no halo, then the wounds are counterfeit.

At the time of examination take a piece of white cloth or paper and dip it in the wine and vinegar you are about to use. If the latter have been tampered with the cloth or paper will change colour.

CHAPTER NINE
De Corporibus Feminarum Inspiciendis

Si quaestio de morte virginis habeatur, primum locum ubi jacebat mortua notare oportebit, quo facto corpus aliorsum auferatur. Tum obstetricem appella, quae ungue medio secto necnon et lana cincto, digitum in vaginam coram omnibus inserat. Si lana sanguine rubido maculata, virgo erat.

Corporibus feminarum inspiciendis, vagina maxima cura scrutari debet, si forte acus vel aliud quoddam acutum hac via in vulvam introductus sit. Vulnus superficiale maculam rubram prope umbilicum efficiet; nulla profundi vestigia.

Feminarum corpora quae, vulnere in pudendis accepto, jamdiu putrida scrutari non possunt, omnia in vertice summo et in osse sacro maculas habebunt.

Scire an sit gravida femina, obstetricem jube ventrem mortuae manu deprimere. Si venter ut lapis aut ferrum durus, gravida est.

Si corpus feminae quae gravida caesa vel parturiens mortua est, in sepulero positum, deinde post multos dies de novo inspiciatur, parturitionem interea sine ullo auxilio perfectum fuisse videbis.

Persaepe accidit viduas et virgines juventa prima vulvae morbo affici; hic post nuptias, harmonia yin et yang confecta, partus forma erumpit, monstrum jam colubri jam alio hujus generis simile, et plerumque a vero partu non sine cura distinguendum. Sunt quae alia horrenda edunt, eadem cura inspicienda.

Ubi parturitio vulneribus accelerata est, foetus aetatem et formam (perfectam vel imperfectam) obstetrix determinet. Nam si foetus formam est imperfectus, massa et praeterea nihil, qua liquefacta nil nisi liquor putridus remanet, parturitio vulneribus accelerata minime potest adjudicari.

Infantem propter matris timorem in vulva mortuum, placenta purpurea et nigra et sanguine maculata et mollis sequetur. Si post partum mortuus est, corpus rubidum, placenta alba. Si post partum ob rein quamdam nefariam vel manu vel pede strangulatus sit, gulam digitis comprimere oportebit: facies vel purpurea et rubra, vel purpurea et nigra erit. Si puer qui ita occisus annorum decem est, ejus manus et pedes luctaminis signa ostendent.

CHAPTER TEN
Dried-up Corpses

First lay down charcoal ash, about the length and breadth of the body in extent; cover it with a piece of thin cloth and sprinkle water all over it. Lay the body on this and cover it entirely with another piece of cloth, on which spread more charcoal ash, covering it once more with cloth, and sprinkling water as before. In a little while the skin and flesh will begin to soften, and then the cloths and ashes can be removed and the body washed with hot vinegar. Spread on the injured parts a mixture of red pepper, onions, salt, and white prunes rubbed down into a poultice with grains and heated over the fire, interposing a sheet of paper between the parts and the poultice. The wounds will then be distinct.

If the wounds have become invisible from the flesh drying, take five catties of grains, powdered ephedra flava, yellow horsetail, and powdered liquorice-root, of each 3 ounces, boil it all into a gruel and let it cool. Then smear it all over the body, make a hole in the ground, and use the steaming process as in winter, heating the ground, throwing plenty of wine and vinegar on, laying the body in, and covering it up with mats, etc. Besides this, take a pot of clean water, pour into it 2 pound of samshoo and boil in it two pieces of cloth. When the corpse is soft remove it into a convenient place and use these to rub it clean: the wounds will then appear.

CHAPTER ELEVEN
Examination of a Decomposed Body

The position of a body having been noted, dash away the maggots and dirt with water, and when the corpse is clean begin to examine. Before applying grains and vinegar, keep on dashing fresh spring water all over the body.

The skin and flesh of wounds inflicted by striking or cutting are of a red colour; if very severe, livid or black; the flesh adheres to the bone and is free from maggots.

Where death has resulted from blows, but decomposition has taken place and the maggots have left nothing but bones, the blood on the wounded part sticks to the bone and dries up black. If there is no wound, but the bone has cracks in it like hairs or like the cracks in china and barely discernible, these are proofs that there was no wound.

Where the body is too much decomposed for examination, you must report clearly that the hair was gone, the skin and flesh on the temples, head, face, and all over the body was livid or black, quite decomposed and eaten away by maggots, so that the bones were exposed.

If the skin and flesh are in a state of decomposition, you must report whether entirely so, round the parts where the bones show, or whether only slightly so on the surface; also, whether there are any other injuries on the body, as also the age of deceased, his facial appearance and the cause of death. Moreover, that the body was really too far gone for examination, and that having felt it all over with your hands you failed to find any broken bones.

CHAPTER TWELVE
Examination of Bones

Man has three hundred and sixty-five bones, corresponding to the number of days it. takes the heavens to revolve.

The skull of a male, from the nape of the neck to the top of the head, consists of eight pieces, of a Ts'ai-chow man, nine. There is a horizontal suture across the back of the skull, and a perpendicular one down the middle. Female skulls are of six pieces, and have the horizontal but not the perpendicular suture.

Teeth are twenty-four, twenty-eight, thirty-two or thirty-six in number. There are three long-shaped breast-bones.

There is one bone belonging to the heart of the shape and size of a cash.

There is one "shoulder-well" bone and one "rice-spoon" bone on either side.

Males have twelve ribs on either side, eight long and four short. Females have fourteen on each side.

Near the kidneys of both males and females there is a bone about as big as the hand perforated with eight holes in rows of two.

The bones in the forearm are two in number as also in the leg between the knee and ankle. At the wrists and ankles of males there are ribs; women have not these. Both knees have a bone hidden inside as big as the thumb. In the hand and foot there are five spaces, the thumb and big toe being each divisible into two parts. These last have each two joints; the other fingers and toes, three.

The pelvic bone is like a pig's kidneys, with the indented part just under the spine. In males, there is quite a curve where the spine meets this bone, making it appear as if there were horns sticking up on either side, like the water caltrop. It has nine holes. In women, the part where the spine joins is flat, and there are only six holes. Take a. thin piece of twine or a strip of bamboo and tie a paper mark to each bone for convenience sake at future examinations, and to prevent confusion.

CHAPTER THIRTEEN
Examination of Bones Long after Death

For the examination of bones the day should be clear and bright. First take clean water, and wash them, and then with string tie them together in proper order so that a skeleton is formed and lay this on a mat. Then make a hole in the ground, 5 ft. long, 3 ft. broad, and 2 ft. deep. Throw into this plenty of firewood and charcoal and keep it burning till the ground is thoroughly hot. Clear out the fire and pour in two pints of good spirit and five pounds of strong vinegar. Lay the bones quickly in the steaming pit and cover well up with rushes, reeds, etc. Let them remain there for two or three hours until the ground is cold, when the coverings may be removed, the bones taken to a convenient spot and examined under a red oil-cloth umbrella.

If the day is dark or rainy the boiling method must be adopted. Take a large jar and heat in it a quantity of vinegar; then having put in plenty of salt and white prunes boil it all together with the bones, superintending the process yourself. When it is boiling fast, take out the bones, wash them in water and hold them up to the light. The wounds will be perfectly visible, the blood having soaked into the wounded parts, marking them with red or dark-blue or black. Next carefully observe if any of the bones are cracked or split.

The above method is, however, not the only one. Take a new yellow oil-cloth umbrella from Hangchow, hold it over the bones and every particle of wound hidden in the bone will be clearly visible.

In cases where the bones are old and the wounds have been obliterated by long exposure to wind and rain, or dulled by frequent boilings, it only remains to examine them in the sun under a yellow umbrella, which will show the wounds as far as possible.

There must be no zinc boiled with the bones or they will become dull.

Where bones have passed several times through the process of examination they become quite white and exactly like uninjured bones; in which case, take such as should show wounds and fill them with oil by the cracks and holes there always are. Wait till the oil is oozing out all over, then wipe it off and hold the bone up to the light; where there are wounds the oil will stop and not pass, the clean parts have not been injured.

Another Method: Rub some good ink thick and spread it on the bone. Let it dry and then wash it off, where there are wounds, and there only, it will sink into the bone.

Another Method: Take some new cotton wool and pass it over the bone. Wherever there is a wound some will be pulled out. At all injured places note whether the splinters of bone point inwards or outwards. In wounds from blows they point inwards; and if they point outwards these are not wounds. Wherever the skull has been hurt the bone is dark-coloured; wherever a bone has been broken, there will be traces of blood on it.

Carefully observe any dark-coloured or purple and black halo-like appearance. If long-shaped, it was inflicted by a weapon of some kind; if round, by the fist; if large, by the head; if small, by the point of the foot.

When the preparing and examination of the bones is finished, the assistants should call them over in order. For instance, that such and such bones are all complete, and so on. Next, let every single bone be marked carefully with a number to facilitate their being put together again (if required). Wrap them up in several folds of paper and three or four folds of oil-paper, tie the packet securely with string, seal and sign it. Then pack it up in a tub, covering the top with a board, make a hole and bury the tub, piling up earth and setting a mark, besides using the lime seal.

Part Two
To Ascertain Whether the Wounds Were Inflicted
Before or after Death

Wounds inflicted on the bone leave a red mark and a slight appearance of saturation, and where the bone is broken there will be at either end a halo-like trace of blood. Take a bone on which there are marks of a wound and hold it up to the light; if these are of a fresh-looking red, the wound was inflicted before death and penetrated to the bone; but if there is no trace of saturation from blood, although there is a wound, it was inflicted after death.

All men have old scars on their bodies, either from falling down in youth or fighting, being bambooed, boils, etc. Although the place heals in time, the scar never passes away; it takes a darkish hue and remains visible after death. For where the blood has once congealed, it will never resume its former appearance. But old wounds have not the halo-like appearance, are soft to the touch, are on a level with the parts surrounding, and of a dull colour. The flesh and bone are both different from those of a recent wound.

CHAPTER FOURTEEN
Anatomy of the Human Body

A mere list of bones.

CHAPTER FIFTEEN
Dropping Blood

The bones of parents may be identified by their children in the following manner. Let the experimenter cut himself or herself with a knife and cause the blood to drip on to the bones; then if the relationship is an actual fact the blood will sink into the bone, otherwise it will not. *Note*: Should the bones have been washed with salt water, even though the relationship exists, yet the blood will not soak in. This is a trick to be guarded against beforehand.

It is also said that if parent and child, or husband and wife, each cut themselves and let the blood drip into a basin of water the two bloods will mix, whereas that of two people not thus related will not mix.

Where two brothers who may have been separated since childhood are desirous of establishing their identity as such, but are unable to do so by ordinary means, bid each one cut himself and let the blood drip into a basin. If they are really brothers the two bloods will coagulate into one; otherwise not. But because fresh blood will always coagulate with the aid of a little salt or vinegar, people often smear the basin over with these to attain their own ends and deceive others: therefore always wash out the basin you are going to use, or buy a new one from a shop. Thus, the trick will be defeated.

The above method of dropping blood on the bones may be used even by a grandchild desirous of identifying the remains of his grandfather; but husband and wife not being of the same flesh and blood, it is absurd to suppose that the blood of one would soak into the bones of the other. For such a principle would apply with still more force to the case of a child who had been suckled by a foster-mother and had grown up indebted to her for half its existence. With regard to the water method, if the basin used is large and full of water the bloods will be unable to mix from being so much diluted; and

43

in the latter case where there is no water, if the interval between dropping the two bloods into the basin is too long, the first will get cold and they will not mix.

CHAPTER SIXTEEN
Examination of Ground

There are some atrocious villains who, when they have murdered any one, burn the body and throw the ashes away, so that there are no bones to examine. In such cases, you must carefully find out at what time the murder was committed and where the body was burnt. Then, when you know the place, all witnesses agreeing on this point, you may proceed without further delay to examine the wounds. The mode of procedure is this: Put up your shed near where the body was burnt, and make the accused and witnesses point out themselves the exact spot. Then cut down the grass, etc. growing on this spot, and burn large quantities of fuel till the place is extremely hot, throwing on several pecks of hemp-seed. By and by brush the place clean, then, if the body was actually burnt on this spot, the oil from the seed will be found to have sunk into the ground in the form of a human figure, and wherever there were wounds on the dead man, there on this figure the oil will be found to have collected together, large or small, square, round, long, short, oblique, or straight, exactly as they were inflicted. The parts where there were no wounds will be free from any such appearances. But supposing you obtain the outline only of the wounds without the necessary detail, then scrape away the masses of oil, light a brisk fire on the form of the body and throw on grains mixed with water. Make the fire burn as fiercely as possible, and throw on vinegar, instantly covering it over with a new well-varnished table. Leave the table on a little while, and then take it off for examination: the form of the body will be transferred to the table, and the scars of the wounds will be distinct in every particular.

If the place is wild, and some time has elapsed since the deed, so that the very murderer does not remember the exact spot, inquire carefully in what direction it was with regard to such and such a village or temple, and how far off. If all agree on this point, proceed in person to the place and bid your assistants go round about searching for any spots where the grass is taller and stronger than usual, marking such with a mark. For where a body has been burnt the grass will be darker in hue, more luxuriant, and taller than that surrounding it, and will not lose these characteristics for a long time, the fat and grease of the body sinking down to the roots of the grass, and causing the above results. If the spot is on a hill or in a wild place where the vegetation is very luxuriant, then you must look for a growth about the height of a man. If the burning took place on stony ground, the crumbly appearance of the stones must be your guide: this makes the process much easier.

TABLE OF CONTENTS
BOOK TWO

CHAPTER ONE.
Death from Blows in a Fight

Where death has resulted from blows in a fight, the mouth and eyes will be open, the hair and clothes disordered, and the two arms stretched out. [For just previous to death the mouth will be in full play, and the eyes will be glaring fiercely; the hair and clothes will get disordered in the scuffle; and the arms, employed in defence, will be stretched out.] Where there are wounds the skin will separate from the membrane below and will sound if tapped by the finger. If hot vinegar is applied, the cicatrix will appear. Observe its size and measure its length and breadth. Also note how many wounds there are, either of which would have caused death, but fix on some one in the most vulnerable part as the mortal one. If death occurs either within or without the limit, it may be that medical aid has been of no avail, or from exposure to the air, in which case the face would be yellow and flabby.

CHAPTER TWO
Wounds Inflicted by the Hand and Foot, or by Weapons

Where there is blood there is a wound, and all such as are not inflicted by the hand or foot are also called wounds from weapons. "Weapons" are not necessarily swords or knives.

Wounds from the hand are mostly about the upper part of the body, the back and chest, or upper ribs, rarely on the lower ribs. Kicks are generally in the pit of the stomach, the ribs, etc. They are indeed found on the upper part of the body, but not unless the victim was lying on the ground. At the examination all those points should be carefully considered, and not merely the size and shape of the wounds. Blows given by the hand or foot or weapons must be on such parts as the head, face, chest, breasts, etc., to be considered as mortal. An arm or leg broken may cause death; there will be a halo round the parts if the wound was inflicted during life. The colour of a wound inflicted by a weapon, the hand, foot, or anything hard, is, if very severe, a dull purple, accompanied by a slight swelling; if less so, purple and red with a slight swelling, purple and red [without any swelling], dark blue, or even only a little discoloured. Wounds from weapons are long-shaped, either oblique or horizontal; from the fist, round; from a kick, larger than those dealt by the fist.

Wounds which occasion death in a couple of days will be somewhat larger than usual; if inflammation sets in badly, death will result in about that time. If death is instantaneous, the wound will be deeper and more severe, the inflammation purple and black, penetrating at once and thus causing death on the spot.

Wounds received by knocking against things are, even though the skin is unbroken, round or with straight outlines. Though the skin should be broken, the wounds will not be deep. Wounds from weapons, or the hand or foot, where the skin is broken but without bleeding, will have a purple and red

49

halo. [Wounds from knocking against things have no halo; those from blows have.]

Wounds from a stick or bludgeon are oblique and long-shaped: one end will be higher than the other. You must be careful to note which end, and also whether the blow was struck from the right or from the left, as the wound must tally with the blow to make the case easy of investigation.

Where a stick or bludgeon has been used, the wounds will generally be on non-fleshy parts, and the victim may die in any time from two hours to ten days. Where harder weapons have been used, causing death, pay still more attention to the severity of the wounds. If there was a bit of a scuffle first, accused catching hold of deceased's hair and then letting out with his hand or foot, the wounds will generally be in some fleshy vital spot. If a mortal wound is given by the foot in some vital spot, see if accused had on shoes or not.

In all cases of kicks, first ask accused what he had on his feet. If common, homemade shoes with soft soles, the wound will be slight and swollen; if shop-made shoes, with sewn soles, the wounds will be more severe and hard. Shoes with sharp-pointed toes will cut into the bone, and nailed shoes will inflict a still heavier wound, discolouring the bone. Wounds which injure the bone most are inflicted by shoes with smooth, round toes, heavily studded with nails. Such require careful discrimination.

Blows given with the head, elbow, knee, &c., must be classed as such according to the evidence, and considered generally as coming under the head of blows from " weapons."

Where wounds are inflicted with weapons and the skin is not broken, but the bone and flesh are injured, or where the wound is in a fleshy place, examination should proceed at once. It will be necessary to elicit clearly whether, if the wound is on the left side, it was inflicted with the right hand, or whether on the right side, and consequently more round towards the back, it was inflicted from behind.

Examine carefully the length, breadth, shape, and size of all wounds inflicted by the hand, foot, or any weapon; also, if the skin is at all broken. Before washing the body, sprinkle them with water, take the heart of an onion, pound it to a pulp and lay it on the injured parts; apply a poultice of grains and vinegar, and in a short time the wounds will be clear and distinct.

A blow from the open hand, though it will not cause death unless on a vital spot, still comes under the heading of "hand." The marks of fingers and a palm will be there, corresponding to the hand. Such are always on the face.

When the instrument of death was a fowling-piece, the aperture of the wound may be examined or even the bones may be examined some time after death. As, however, the belly and bowels soon decompose, and there is no basis of operations in such a case, take what decomposed flesh there is in the coffin and wash it out with water. If the wound was a gun-wound, there will be shot in it, though you must be very careful that none are inserted purposely by interested parties.

CHAPTER THREE
Wounds from Wooden and Metal Weapons, Brickbats

Long-shaped, oblique wounds on the bone may be set down to wooden weapons; round wounds with jagged edges, and stab-like three-cornered wounds, to brickbats and tiles. If, however, the wound is oblong, round, oval, etc., the bone smashed and marked with blood, soaking into the middle or even right through to the other side, the colour deep red, approaching to purple and sometimes dark blue or black, then the weapon used was of metal. Such weapons are of various kinds, as life-preservers, knuckledusters, iron hands [holding a sharp iron rod pointed like a pencil], shooting stars [i.e. a piece of iron at the end of a string], but the wounds inflicted are similar in character, piercing right into the bone and very severe, not like wounds from wooden weapons, or the hand, foot, etc., which barely reach the bone.

Further, if the bone is broken into irregular splinters and of a light red or red hue, the wound was inflicted by a wooden weapon; but if the splinters are of equal length, broken into an angle one side with the other, and of a dark red or purple hue, the wound was given with some iron weapon.

CHAPTER FOUR
Death from Kicks

Kicks in the pudenda which cause death may be examined if the corpse is not decomposed, though from the very position of such wounds the examination is less likely to be searching and minute. There is, however, a "bone method " which may be adopted, although there are actually no bones in these parts, and such as there are [in proximity] do not show the wounds. To depend, indeed, on the evidence of the bone immediately below the wound would be to let many criminals slip through the meshes of the law. Where wounds have been thus inflicted, no matter whether on man or woman, the wounds will be visible on the upper half of the body and not on the lower. For instance, they will appear in a male at the roots of either the top or bottom teeth, inside; on the right hand if the wound was on the left, and vice versa; in the middle if the wound was central. In women, the wounds will appear on the gums, right or left as above.

Regarding mortal wounds in the upper or lower abdomen, if in the former, and the flesh is decomposed, you must examine the bone with the square holes, which should be red and purple; if the lower abdomen, examine as for the pudenda.

CHAPTER FIVE
Wounds from Knives

In cases of death from knives, etc., before you arrive at the place of examination, ask your informant (the plaintiff) whether the criminal is caught and what class of man he is, what weapon he used and whether it has been secured. If it has, cause it to be produced that you may note its size, and draw a facsimile of it on paper. If it has not been secured, ask plaintiff where it is and make him draw it and sign his name below the drawing. Also, be very careful to ask if accused is a relative of deceased, and if there was any ill-feeling between them.

Where death has resulted from wounds with knives, etc., the mouth and eyes will be open, the hair disordered, and the hands slightly clenched. The mortal wound will be the largest and longest, the skin shrunk and the flesh exposed; if the belly is cut open the bowels will protrude.

When the murdered man saw his slayer about to strike him with a knife, he naturally stretched forth his hand to ward off the blow; on his hand, therefore, there will be a wound. If, however, the murderer struck him in some fleshy vital part and killed him with one blow, he will have no wound on his hand, but the death-wound will be severe. A cut on the head will sever the hair as if with a knife or scissors. If the skull is fractured at the crown, it was done by some sharp-pointed weapon; this [the fracture] you must ascertain by pressing down the bone with your finger. A wound from a pointed knife or chopper will be wide at the mouth and narrow inside: a shallow wound from a sword will be narrow, a deep one broad. A wound from the edge of a sword or knife will be narrow at both ends, there being no extraordinary pressure exerted at either. A shallow spear-wound will be narrow, a deep one round, from the spear-handle having penetrated. Suppose the weapon was a bamboo spear or a sharp pointed coolie's pole used against a vital part, the mouth of the wound will be jagged and irregular. Such scars may be of almost any shape. Where

54

death has resulted from a wound with a sharp weapon, the clothes of deceased must be examined to see if there is a cut, and if the blood stain corresponds with the position of the wound. Where from a knife wound the bowels protrude there will be several cuts upon them. But, it may be asked, how can one blow produce several cuts? Evidently from the peculiar arrangement of the bowels coiled up as they are in the abdomen.

Where death has resulted from blows with weapons, if the weapon was sharp pointed the wound will have been a stab, but if blunt, not a stab. If the wound was given on the belly, it will be necessary to give the length, breadth, and depth of the wound. If the membrane is pierced and the bowels protrude, there being congealed blood, such a wound was the direct cause of death. So also for the pit of the stomach and the ribs. So too for the throat when the wound has reached and injured the bone, and the parts round about are irregularly lacerated, and the gullet and wind-pipe severed. A wound on the top of the head, or on the temples, or on the back of the head, it would take a heavy, sharp weapon to break the bone; with blood accompanying the scattered brains, must be regarded as a mortal wound, and the actual
cause of death.

Wounds are generally inflicted face to face, the weapon being held in the right hand, and are generally inflicted on the left side. For unless held horizontally, the point of the sword could not first come in contact with the right side; but supposing it did, this would be evident from the character of the wound. If the striker is left-handed the wound will be on the right. If it is a case of a sleeping man being wounded, note first the entrance to his sleeping apartment and how the bed was placed. Inquire how deceased was in the habit of lying, and which way his head and feet pointed, and then proceed to examine according to the answers.

Where a man strikes with the hand he is not daily accustomed to use, the blow will fall too high or too low, and will not be even and straight. For instance, a man who is in the habit of using his right hand strikes with his left at the neck of a man lying the wrong way for him, the point of the sword will fall a little too low and slightly wound the right shoulder. [A case is given in the notes of a coroner who fixed on the actual murderer of a man killed in a junk-fight, by making all engaged in the brawl eat before him. When they had finished their meal he dismissed them with the exception of one, to whom he cried in a voice of thunder, "You are the man! Deceased was killed by a wound on his right side, and you alone ate your rice with your left hand." The murderer confessed.]

Where from lapse of time the knife used shows no stains, heat it red hot in a charcoal fire and pour on it some first-rate vinegar, the marks of blood will then appear.[An instance is given in the notes of a murder being cleared up in the following manner: The coroner who had identified the wounds as inflicted by a sickle, and had found out that a certain man had quarrelled with deceased about a loan of money, went to the village where the suspected man lived and caused every man to produce his sickle laying them on the ground before him. In a little while he turned to the suspected man and accused him of the murder. He denied his guilt with many protestations, but the coroner pointed to the flies which had singled out his sickle among seventy others, attracted by the smell of blood. The murderer confessed.]

Part Two
To Distinguish Knife Wounds
Given Before and after Death

In examining knife-wounds, the first point is to ascertain clearly if they were inflicted by the edge [i.e. not the point] and also, whether before or after death. A wound inflicted with the edge of the knife before death will be gaping and irregular in its formation; clean, regular wounds may be regarded as inflicted after death. Wounds inflicted before death will be characterized by the presence of clotted blood, and by the fresh-looking appearance of the blood and flesh at the mouth of the wound, death being caused by the rupture of the membrane. The flesh of wounds inflicted after death will be dry and white; there will not be the same appearance of the blood.

Where knife-wounds have been received while life was present, the skin and flesh will shrink; there will be a subcutaneous stain all round. Wherever a limb has been cut off, the muscles, bone, skin, and flesh will be in a sticky mass; the skin shrunk from contact with the blade and the bone protruding. Where a corpse has been cut to pieces the skin and flesh will not change in appearance, there will be no subcutaneous stain, the skin will not have shrunk, there will be no blood at the end of the wound, and it will be of a white colour. If the wound is washed and the two sides pressed together with the fingers and no clear blood flows from it, the wound was not inflicted during life. Where decapitation has been performed during life, the muscles will have shrunk inwards, the skin curled up, and the bone will protrude; the shoulders also will be higher. Performed after death, the neck will become elongated, the skin will not shrink, the bone protrude, or the shoulders become higher.

When it is a case of a body the head and trunk of which are in different places, first make the relatives identify the corpse, and when you have taken its exact position measure how far from the head or feet.

57

In case of mutilation of limbs, when you have measured how far each is from the body and taken notes accordingly, put all the parts together complete and lay the corpse in a coffin, comparing a few of the limbs with the stumps to see that they agree. If the flesh is not red and if, although there may be the appearances of wounds, there is no blood and marrow, your verdict must be that the mutilation was inflicted after death when the blood had ceased to circulate.

CHAPTER SIX
Suicide with Knives

In cases of inquests on suicides, begin by asking your original informant what class of man deceased was, at what time he committed suicide, and what kind of weapon he used. If anyone comes to identify the corpse ask deceased's age and whether when alive he was right or left-handed. If he was a slave, cause the bill of sale, etc., to be produced. Ask too if he has any relatives and whether he was right or left-handed. The wounds also must be carefully examined as to whether they were inflicted before or after death; in the former case there will have been a flow of blood, in the latter case not.

If the throat was cut by the suicide himself before death, the mouth and eyes will be closed and the two hands clenched; the flesh will be yellow and the hair in order; there will be a wound on the neck of a certain length and breadth; the windpipe and gullet will be severed.

The mouth and eyes of all who cut through the lower part of their own throats are closed; their hands are clenched and their arms drawn up closely. The colour of the flesh is yellow and the hair undisturbed.

A small knife will inflict a wound from 1 in. to 2 in. long, a cooking-knife from 3 in. to 4 in. or thereabouts. If crockery is used the wound will be small, though a wound from any sharp-edged weapon will cause death if the windpipe is cut, no matter how slightly. Cuts from sharp weapons on the throat, pit of the stomach, abdomen, ribs, temples, crown of the head and such vital spots, even though not of large size, will cause death if the membrane is pierced. If on the other hand such wounds are not deep, even though there may be several, death will not ensue.

If the left hand is used the wound will begin from behind the right ear, extending from one to two inches on the other side of the throat, and vice versa. The beginning of the wound will be of a severer character than the end. [Pain will cause the suicide to relax his grip.]

Where the suicide has cut his throat with one cut and died on the spot the wound will be nearly 2 in. deep, both gullet and windpipe severed; if he lingers a day, about 12 in., the gullet severed and the windpipe slightly injured; if death results after three days only the gullet will have been severed, the wound being about 18 in. deep, the hair will be in disorder, and there will not be more than one wound, the suicide not being able to inflict a second. If the hair is in disorder, the wound irregular, with no distinction between its depth at one end and the other, the case is one of murder.

Where the throat has been cut with a knife, the characteristics vary, noticeably in the mouth and eyes. Where suicide was committed in an outbreak of passion, the teeth will be firmly set, the eyes slightly open and looking upwards, from the angry feelings excited. If committed through excess of pent-up rage, the eyes will be closed, but not tightly, the mouth slightly open, and the teeth in the majority of cases not shut, arising from the disturbed state of the mind up to the last moment. If driven to commit suicide from a fear of punishment, the eyes of the dead man will be closed, as also his mouth, for he looks on death merely as a return home and a happy release from the responsibilities of life. If such be the case, inquire carefully whether his disposition while alive was rough or gentle, distinguishing between the three periods of youth, manhood, and old age.

The right hand of a man who cut his throat with that hand will be soft, and one or two days after death will curl up, but the left hand will not curl up, and vice versa. Where death was caused by another person neither hand will curl up.

Where a man has cut off his own hand or a finger the flesh and skin will be evenly cut, and if properly bandaged will not cause death immediately, but such a result will be from want of taking due precautions. The flesh and skin about such a

60

wound will curl inwards, but not if the wound was inflicted after death.

A finger bitten off by oneself will generally cause death because of the poison in the teeth. All round the wound where the bone is broken there will be a quantity of matter; the skin and flesh will be rotten, and death will result from the impossibility of a cure. There will be marks of teeth, and a generally uneven appearance.

CHAPTER SEVEN
Suicide by Strangulation

At an inquest on a suicide by strangulation, begin by asking where, in what street, and in whose house it occurred, what persons saw it, what was used to consummate the act, where the body was suspended, and whether a running or tight noose was tied. Then examine whether deceased's clothes are old or new, measure the position of the corpse, noting which way the face and back pointed, and what deceased stood upon. Measure the distance between the head and whatever the body may be suspended from, as well as that between the feet and the ground. In case of the place of suicide being low, measure the distance between whatever the rope was attached to and the ground. Cut the body down before the assembled people, and carry it to a place where there is plenty of light; then only may you cut the rope from the body, measuring its entire length and the length of the part round the neck; also the circumference of deceased's neck, noting the exact position of the scar. This done proceed to examination.

Begin by asking the original informant what class of man the deceased was, whether he committed suicide early or late in the day, and whether he was cut down in the hope of saving his life; also whether his death was reported early or late. If any one identifies the body, ask him deceased's age, and what was his occupation, what family he had, and what was his reason for committing this act. If deceased was a slave cause his master to produce the documents to that effect, and see if any relatives are mentioned therein, as also his age. Observe carefully the place where deceased committed suicide, and, if already cut down, ask whether when cut down life was extinct or not; also, how much time has elapsed since. Be careful, too, to ascertain accurately the height of the beam. If the feet dangle in the air, the tongue protrude, and the scar round the neck is not a circle, return a verdict of suicide from strangulation, the characteristics being distinct from those of murder.

In examining a case of strangulation where the body is still hanging, notice first the distance from the ground and from what it may be suspended, also whether the latter would be sufficiently strong for such a purpose. If the body is not actually suspended, note what there is under its feet, what kind of rope was used, and the circumference and diameter of the noose; also observe the breadth of the scar on the neck before cutting down the body and taking it away for examination. If the body has been already taken down, ask if the rope or whatever was used is still on the neck of the deceased or near the body or in the place where the act was committed, for the rope should be carefully compared with the scar. If the weather was wet and muddy, note what deceased had on his feet, and if whatever he stood upon is marked accordingly.

In cases of suicide by strangulation the two eyes will be closed, the lips and mouth black, and the teeth slightly showing. If the rope was above the *Adami pomum* the mouth will be tightly closed, the teeth firmly set, and the tongue pressed against the teeth but not protruding; but if below, the mouth will be open, and about one-third of tongue protruding, the face will be of a purple-red, at the corners of the mouth and on the chest there will be frothy saliva; the hands will be clenched, the thumbs and toes pointing downwards, and there will be marks on the legs as from cauterization; the abdomen will be pendulous and of a livid or black colour, etc., the scar on the neck will be purple and red, or black, as if from a bruise, extending from the back of one ear to the back of the other, and measuring fronm 9 in. to 1 ft. and upwards.

If deceased's feet were off the ground, the scar under the Adam's apple will be deep; otherwise not so deep. It will be deep if deceased was fat and the rope thin; less so if he was thin or the rope thick. Where a rope of calico or cloth is used the scar will be spread over a larger surface. If the body was

63

hanging at an acute angle with the ground [feet touching, of course], or lying on the ground, the scar will be oblique, not reaching to the hair at the back.

Whatever kind of knot is used it will be necessary to observe what deceased stood upon, and whether when the noose was made there would be enough rope over.

With a running or tight knot death may result if the feet touch the ground, even if the knees touch; with the single-twist cross knot the feet must be entirely off the ground. The single-twist cross knot is used when deceased first tied the rope round his neck and then attaches it to something high up; it will be necessary to observe the dust on whatever that was, and also to note what deceased stood upon, and whether he could have reached up to attach the rope himself. Observe carefully if the rope be stretched or not, and that there is at least a foot between deceased's head and the beam. For if the head be close up against whatever it may be, the feet dangling in the air, and there is nothing deceased could have stood upon, then the hanging of the body was the act of some other person.

Where, in a case of self-strangulation, there is no mark of the knot, it will be because deceased first wound the rope several times round his own neck and then, attaching it to something high, let himself swing till he died. Or else when he had suspended the rope, he hanged himself in a double noose, standing on something high, and thrusting his head into the noose, with an extra turn or so round his neck. The scar resulting, therefore, will be double, the top scar passing upwards from behind the ear towards the hair without crossing, the lower one encircling the neck. Such distinctions should be carefully drawn in reporting the case.

Where there is no mark of a knot on the throat of a suicide by strangulation, there will be in the middle of the scar, on either side of the chin, a faint mark extending towards the ears on either side, with a tendency to diminish gradually the higher it gets. Where a single cord has been used, there will be on either side of the knot a subcutaneous appearance of blood rising obliquely upwards and continuous, not extending in a straight line backwards.

After suspension, circulation ceases, and the body becomes purple and black like collected clouds, or as if in a state of decomposition, but differing in appearance from a red and livid body swollen from beating, or one discoloured in large patches from the effects of poison. In an old or emaciated man this would be less apparent.

Where there has been long illness without hope of recovery and a desire to die as soon as possible, and the sick man lying on his back strangles himself with a rope or girdle, the eyes will be closed, the teeth showing, a small portion of the tongue will protrude, bitten by the teeth, the colour of the flesh will be yellow, the body thin, the hands clenched, etc. The rope or whatever was used will probably be found grasped by the hand of the suicide, the distance of which one from the other must be accurately measured. The scar round the neck will be purple and red, a foot or more in length; the knot will be on the lower part of the throat, and the scar will be deepest in front. If the rope has been already cut away, the belly of the corpse will have swelled, and the tongue will not be bitten.

Beneath the spot where suicide has been committed by hanging, dig a hole three or more feet in depth; if charcoal is present, that was the place. [The note says this results from the natural influence of the dead body over the ground, and must not be regarded as anything extraordinary.]

Where suicide was committed in a room, observe carefully the dust on the beam or whatever the rope was attached to. If it is much scattered, this may be considered in most cases as bona-fide evidence of suicide; but if there is only a single rope-mark, a contrary conclusion follows.

Where suicide was committed in a low place, the body will generally be in a recumbent position, either on its side or face. If the former, the scar will be oblique but horizontal beneath the neck; if the latter, the scar will be straight up from beneath the throat, reaching from behind one ear to the back of the other, but not extending to the hair.

Tap lightly with a stick on the suspending rope; if it is tight, the case is one of suicide; if loose, the body has been hung up there by others. Generally, when a body has been thus brought from elsewhere and hung up, there are two scars, the old one being purple and red with a subcutaneous appearance of blood, the other white without that appearance. The purple and red scar will also be deep, though instances occur of depth unaccompanied by the purple and red discolouration. A white scar is, however, unmistakable evidence of the body being removed from elsewhere.

In cases where from lapse of time the body has become decomposed and the head alone remains attached to the rope, the body having fallen to the ground and the bones become exposed from the rotting of the flesh, it only remains to see whether the rope is in the channel beneath the jaws and whether the two wrists and the bones of the forehead are red. If so, it is a case of suicide.

CHAPTER EIGHT
Strangulation with Violence Passed off as Suicide

Wherever a man has been strangled or otherwise killed, and it is pretended that he committed suicide by hanging, the eyes and mouth will be open, the hands apart, the hair in disorder, circulation will have stopped in the lower part of the throat, the scar will be shallow and faint-coloured, the tongue will not protrude or even be pressed against the teeth, the flesh on the neck will show marks of finger-nails and elsewhere on the body there will be mortal wounds.

Where the victim was half-strangled and then hung up, there will be two scars, one deep and the other shallow, very like in appearance to those which a suicide himself may cause by giving the rope an extra turn round his neck, though the latter are both deep; but in this case the scars are half red and half white and the subcutaneous appearance of blood is not similar.

Wherever a man has been strangled from behind something, as a window or a tree, the same being passed off as suicide, the rope will not have crossed, the scar on the throat will be regular but deep and of a dull black colour, and not beginning behind the ears, etc. Where a man has been strangled on the lower part of his throat, the knot will be at the back of his neck, his two hands will not hang down, or at any rate not straight down. Strangling from behind is generally against a pillar or something of the kind, and often with a piece or part of some garment, the mark being left on the lower part of the throat which, being a vital spot, death ensues from the stoppage of respiration.

Where murder has been committed by strangulation, the rope having been passed several times round deceased's neck, the knot will generally be at the back in the middle or slightly inclined to either side; there will be some rope over, hanging down, and the corpse will be lying on its face. From the struggle which he made for his life, deceased's hair will be in disorder, and over his body will be found the marks of bruises, scuffling, etc.

Where the hands, feet or neck of corpse have been tied round with rope, because the man is already dead and circulation has stopped, there will be no subcutaneous appearance of blood, and although the cords have penetrated deeply, the scar will not be livid or red, but white.

Where a scar has been burnt in with a hot iron, the mark will be red or scorched and moist.

Where a man has been beaten and finally killed by strangulation, there will be a dark mark on the lower part of the throat, six or seven inches long, not reaching to the back of the neck.

Where a man has been strangled in the ordinary way, there will be a black scar all round the throat over a foot in length.

Sometimes a man is strangled on another's back [the rope being over the murderer's shoulder], in which case there will be traces of the rope having been crossed, the scar will be straight towards the back of the neck, the extremities falling a little and gradually shading off, and generally on the lower part of the throat, not on the chin or under jaws. For in strangling a man over the shoulder on the back, unless the feet are raised off the ground, death would not immediately ensue.

CHAPTER NINE
Death from Drowning

In cases of death from drowning, begin by asking the original informant if it was early or late when he saw the body in the water, and whether it was in the very spot it now is, or whence it has just been taken, or whether it floated down from elsewhere and if so from what direction and how it came to stop in this place. If witness says he saw deceased fall into the water, ask whether he pulled him out or not and, if he did so whether he reported the case instantly or after some delay.

If, either in a river or a lake, it is difficult to take the proper measurements as to the position of the body, observe the spot where it was floating; if it was not floating but raised and taken out, inquire for the spot whence it was thus raised. Pools or pits with water in them deep enough to drown people, should be fathomed in order to get the depth, and their position should be taken; moreover, wherever a body is found floating or is thrown up in river or stream, lake or pond, the name of the place should be ascertained as well as that of the tenant or occupier.

Where a body has been many days in the water it will have swelled up and the direct cause of death will not be distinct. In such cases report that the hair has fallen off, the skin peeled off, that the head is swollen, the lips are turned back and opened, the skin and flesh over the whole body is livid or black; and let your verdict be that these appearances arise from being so long in the water, well or rive, as the case may be; that you have found traces of froth in the mouth and nose of deceased, that the abdomen has swelled up, and that whether or no there are any other injuries on the body there is no evidence to show.

In the case of the body of a drowned man, where it is no question of blows, having on the head or face wounds from sharp weapons, it will be necessary to empty out the water in

69

order to see if there is any sharp thing, either metal or crockery, against which he might have struck. For striking against any such thing before life was extinct would cause a flow of blood, and the wound would closely resemble one inflicted before death, which mistake however, must be carefully guarded against. So also for suicides in wells.

If it is a case of a slave or a wife who before throwing herself into the water received wounds from beating, in pronouncing a verdict of accidental death or suicide, etc., it will be necessary to enter the wounds in the prescribed form, noting that they were inflicted before deceased jumped into the water. Bodies take a long time to float in the cold weather at the beginning of spring, a shorter time in spring, summer, and towards the end of autumn.

If examination be delayed and the corpse is exposed to wind and sun, the skin all over it will rise and form into white blisters.

Where the water is at all deep and broad, the suicide or murdered man as the case may be, will show no bruises from striking against anything; but if the place be shallow and narrow, the result will be similar to jumping or being pushed into a well. Generally speaking, water three or four feet in depth is enough to drown people, and if there is no other apparent cause, your verdict may be "Death by drowning." But if there is a rope attached to the body or any other suspicious appearances, then it is a case of murder rather than suicide.

If deceased slipped and fell into the water, the mouth and eyes will be both open, the hands will not be clenched, and if the place was narrow, there will be wounds on the head and face.

Where suicide by drowning is committed in consequence of illness, the depth of the water is an unimportant matter as almost any depth would cause death. There will be no other marks about the body, except a slight yellowness in colour. Where from illness deceased fell into a ditch and was

70

drowned, the mouth and eyes will be open, and the hands slightly clenched. Wash the parts which have been in the water and mud first with water, and then spurt wine over them from the mouth. The flesh will be rather white, the skin of the abdomen slightly swelled, and mud in the finger-nails which will not come out with washing.

An old man may be held under water and so suffocated, but in this case there will be no marks on the body and the belly will not swell.

Part Two
To Distinguish Between Bodies of Drowned Persons, and Those Thrown in after Death.

The body of a drowned man floats on its face (it is curious to note that the contrary belief prevailed among the ancients) though not if there is any silver money about it; the body of a woman floats on its back with the face looking upwards, the hands and feet pointing forwards, the mouth closed, the eyes either open or shut, the belly swelled, and sounding if struck with the hand. [Where deceased fell into the water, the hands will be open, the eyes slightly open, and the skin of the abdomen slightly swelled up; but if he jumped into the water, the hands will be clenched, the eyes closed, and the bowels much swelled.] The skin beneath the feet will be white and wrinkled, the hair not in any way loose. Both the head and hair as well as the fingernails and toe-nails, or if shoes were worn, these as well, will be full of sand and mud. [The note says sand and mud are sucked into the nose and mouth of a drowning man by his efforts to draw breath, which of course is not the case with a body thrown into the water after death.] If in the nose and mouth there is froth, and faint traces of blood specks, or if there are any marks of injuries from striking against anything, these are evidences of death from drowning.

If death was the result of illness and the body was subsequently thrown into the water, there will be no traces of

71

froth in the nose or mouth, and there being no water in the belly it will not be swelled up. The face will be slightly yellow, and the body thin.

Where a man has been killed by blows and then thrust into the water, the colour of his flesh will be rather yellow than white, the mouth and eyes open, his arms stretched out, his hair in disorder, the skin of the abdomen will not have swelled up, no water will flow either from the mouth, eyes, ears, or nose, there will be no sand or mud in the finger-nails, the hands will not be clenched, the soles of the feet will not be wrinkled or white but puffed out, and the mortal wounds on the body will be of a black colour. Some corpses are fat and others lean; observe this at the time of examination, and take note of any wounds there may be, for the presence of such, even though it be a case of suicide, renders a careful investigation imperative.

If there are no traces of wounds on the body, but the face is purple or red and the mouth and eyes open, death resulted from deceased being held in the water by his feet, with his head downwards.

CHAPTER TEN
Death by Drowning in a Well

In cases of drowning in wells begin by asking the original informant why, when he first saw there was somebody in the well, he did not attempt a rescue; and how, before the body floated, he knew there was one there at all. If the well is one attached to the house ask how, deceased being missing the whole day, he came to know he was in the well. Wherever there is a man in a well, the fact will be first apparent by there being frothy bubbles on the surface, and this may serve as a guide in investigations. Take the exact position of the well, the name of the man on whose ground it is and the name of the place. If the body was found at the bottom of the well it will not be necessary to take the position, but only to get an approximate measurement of the depth before taking out the body.

A body in a well which has swelled up will show about a foot out of water, but this will not be the case if the water is shallow. If there is any part above water, observe whether the head is uppermost or the feet, and measure accordingly; but if not, then with the measuring rod take the distance down to the body, noting also whether the head is uppermost or the feet.

Wherever any one has jumped, been pushed, or fallen into a well, there will be wounds on the head from striking against or grazing the bricks, his finger-nails will be full of sand and mud, his belly swelled, and if laid on his side or face, water will come out of his mouth. Where a man has been pushed or fallen into a well, his hands will be stretched out, his eyes partly open, and perhaps he may have money about him or valuables, but if he jumped in to commit suicide, his eyes will be closed, his hands clenched, and there will be no money about his person.

Suicides generally jump in feet first; the contrary is the result of falling in under pursuit or being pushed in. Where a

73

man has slipped and fallen into a well, his mouth and eyes will be open. Carefully observe the marks on the ground where he slipped.

In the 5th and 6th moons there is, both in wells and in grave mounds, foul air destructive to human life, and when in summer or autumn, the water being gone, men descend to clean out these wells, death is often the result of inhaling this poisonous air. This fact must be kept in mind at inquests on suicides.

CHAPTER ELEVEN
Death by Burning

In cases of death by burning, begin by asking the original informant where the fire began, where deceased was at the time and why; also whether any assistance was rendered to him, and whether he had had any fight or quarrel with another person. When all this is clear, you may proceed to examination. It may happen that the hair is burnt up, the head and entire trunk are scorched black, and that it is impossible to say whether or not there may be on the body any other causes of death, or to specify deceased's death and facial appearance. State clearly whether in the mouth or nose there is any trace of ashes, for this is the crucial test of death by burning.

In examining a body where death has resulted from burning, first observe if there are tiles, straw, and ashes beneath it or not; for where a man has been burned in a house roofed with tiles or straw, the body will be found underneath these, whereas if he has been forced in by another man out of revenge, etc., his body will be found uppermost. Also note the direction of the head and feet.

Where a body has been burnt to cinders and there is nothing left to examine, take the evidence of your assistants and the neighbours to that effect; then having closely investigated the circumstances of the burning, report that nothing of the body remains for examination, and determine the case according to the evidence.

Part Two
To Distinguish Between Bodies Burnt
Before and after Death

Where the burning took place before death, there will be in the mouth and nose of the deceased a sooty-like ash; the hands and feet will be drawn up. If burning after death, although the hands and feet will be drawn up, there will be no ashes in the mouth; and if the elbows and knees are not burnt, the arms and legs will not be drawn up.

It is a common saying that muscles are the connecting links in the human body, and this is more than ever true of their relation to the bones. Corpses of persons who have been burnt are indeed generally found upon their faces, but if burnt upon the back the corpse rises into a sitting posture from the contraction of the muscles, often frightening people thus. Therefore the fact of the hands and feet being drawn up is not sufficient guarantee that the body was burnt either before or after death; but as a general principle it may be held that if the colour of the body after burning is scorched and black, death had already taken place, and that if the bones are yellow and greasy death resulted from the burning.

The bones of a man who has been burnt to death will sound if let fall; those of a corpse burnt after death will not.

If fire be applied to wounds the skin will not blister; the flesh beneath will be purple and red.

Where an invalid of long standing has been accidentally burnt to death, the colour of the flesh will be scorched and black, and the flesh itself perhaps shrivelled up; the hands and arms will be drawn up on the breast, the knees also drawn up, the eyes and mouth open, or perhaps the teeth clenched or biting the lips; there will be a yellowish fat bursting through the skin and flesh.

Where a man has been strangled and subsequently thrown into the fire, his hair will be scorched and yellow, his head and whole body scorched black, his skin and flesh shrivelled; there will be no watery blisters or broken places on his body. On the lower part of the throat there will be the marks of strangling.

If deceased was killed with some sharp-edged weapon, and it is pretended that he was burnt to death, bid your assistants pick up the bones and sweep up the ashes and dust. Then upon the clean spot where the body lay sprinkle the whey

76

of grains and vinegar, and if deceased was murdered with a knife or similar weapon there will be a fresh coloured bloodstain where the blood soaked into the ground. But first ask where deceased slept the last night of his life, for fear the body might have been moved after death, in which case there would be some difficulty in basing a decision on such evidence.

In cases of death from burning, wherever the victim fell there will be below the surface the outline of his body. It will be necessary to sweep away the ashes, etc., from the spot, sprinkle vinegar and cover it over for a little while with mats, when it will appear to view. Where a man has been strangled, and thrown into a fire, the inside of his throat will not be burnt, the scar will preserve it. Where a man has been killed with a knife or similar instrument, there will be blood on the ground. The place must be swept and vinegar sprinkled, when a fresh-coloured red will be the result.

CHAPTER TWELVE
Death from Scalding

In cases of wounds from scalds the skin and flesh of deceased will be broken, the skin peeled off and white, showing white flesh below. The flesh generally will be rotten and red.

In most cases of scalding and burning the wounds are on the victim's hands, feet, or breast. If any blows were struck, or he was knocked into the hot water or fire with the head, the foot, or the hand, the wounds will be on the back of either forearm, or on the thighs, &c. Blisters will not rise on injured parts, which are quite different from scalds, etc.

Scalds, unless over the heart before or behind, are not mortal. They are principally on the head and ribs, the hands and feet, more severe in some parts and less so in others. Self-inflicted scalds are chiefly on the hands and feet, the chest and upper part of the back.

A corpse which has been scalded turns white, but is not otherwise affected; neither do blisters rise on it.

BOOK III

CHAPTER ONE
Miscellaneous Remarks on Suspicious Appearances

At an inquest regard nothing unimportant. The adage says:

A difference of a hair will be
The difference of a thousand li.

For often it is difficult to tell whether a man has been strangled or whether he committed suicide by hanging himself; whether he was accidentally drowned or threw himself into the water; whether he died from the effects of blows received or fell a victim to disease. Besides which, slaves frequently commit suicide in one way or another in consequence of being beaten, etc., necessitating a prompt and searching investigation into the ever-varying circumstances which thus create suspicion.

In examining a corpse bearing suspicious marks upon it, if the weapon was sharp-edged and penetrated right through, note both where it went and that where it came out. If the body is decomposed, compare the position of the wound on the body with the mark on the clothes deceased was wearing. Suppose deceased to be lying on his face and with some short weapon or a pointed piece of bamboo in his hand, in certain cases it is quite possible he may have fallen down in a fit of drunkenness and inflicted the wounds on himself. If he is lying near some high place or in mud, examine carefully if there are any other marks or any money about the body or signs of injuries whatsoever.

Where a man has been killed, but from lapse of time the body has decomposed and there remains nothing certain to go by, examine the bone between the top of the head and the forehead, commonly called "the cover of the mind." This will have started up, leaving a slight fissure, and will be of a faint red or livid colour, caused by the rush of blood thither in

79

consequence of the stoppage of respiration. Examination of this bone will make the case clear.

The "door of life" bone is very tender, and death may result from its being struck by the hand. For on either side of it there are two holes through which runs a red muscle as thin as silk connecting the two kidneys; death would ensue if this were broken, but there would be no trace of the injury on the surface of the body. If death is stated to have been caused by striking the "door of life," examine the bone, which in such case should be purple and red. The "door of life" bone extends from the os sacrum upwards to the seventh joint in the spine; there is a small hole on either side by which it may be known.

In all cases where there are no marks of wounds, but the face is of a dull, livid colour, and perhaps looking as if was swelled on one side, you may be almost sure that death was the result of something being pressed over the mouth and nose, or from strangulation with a handkerchief, girdle, or something of that kind, there being, consequently, no wounds visible. Observe if the skin on the neck is hard or not, as this a very important place; also if the hands and feet show any signs of being tied, the tongue of being bitten, the pudenda, etc., of being stamped upon. If you find none of these marks, then see if there is any saliva in the mouth, and if the neck is swollen or not. If there is saliva accompanied by swelling, death was probably the result of diphtheria, or perhaps occurred in a fit of drunkenness.

It often happens that a man after fighting and separating goes either to wash his face or get a drink in whatever river, pond or pool may be near, and then from sheer exhaustion, sometimes from drunkenness which in the first instance caused him to fight, gets giddy, slips and falls, into the water and is drowned. As he was alive when he fell into the water, the abdomen will swell, there will be sand and mud in his finger nails, and his two arms will be stretched forward; these are evidences of death by drowning, and, although wounds may be found on the body which must be entered on the form, your verdict should be Death by Drowning after a fight. For although the wounds may be on vital spots, there still remains the death-limit, and death from other causes outside the death-limit, both of which come under the head of death from wounds; but in the present case death was the result of falling into the water, and, although there are wounds, must be considered as proceeding from other causes. Further, it very frequently happens that subsequent to a fight a man falls down in getting up on to some high place and is killed. Examine the height of the place, and whether the injuries which resulted are or are not on vital spots. Also closely question those who saw the fight and its termination.

Where a man dies in consequence of blows received in a fight but has no wounds visible, it may be that he was suffering from a disease of long standing, or had taken too much to drink before he began to fight, and then from striking against something during the fight, injured himself so that he died.

Si res ita se habeat, testes ambo in uterum contracti non poterunt cerni. Linum sume calido aceto mersum, quod super infimam abdominis partem spatium caenae imponas. Hoc facto et abdomine manu oppresso, testes statim descendent. Si senex et aegrotus qui ita pugna occisus est, vulneribus non apparentibus, scrotum maxima cura inspicere debet; nam saepe unus tantum testis in uterum contrahitur, qui abdomine manu oppresso statim descendet.

In cases where there are no marks of injuries and no signs of illness, making it very difficult to arrive at any verdict, the chances are that some sharp weapon will have been passed through the crown of the head and perhaps into the brain, thus causing death.

When the relatives and witnesses have drawn up their statements of the case, proceed to cut off deceased's hair and examine.

81

Examine the teeth, tongue, ears and nose of murdered men, as well as the nails on their hands and feet, to see if anything sharp has been thrust into them.

In all cases where your verdict is death by poison, self-strangulation, or jumping into water after being beaten, it is necessary to make a searching personal examination. If it is a case of poison being put in the mouth of a man who has been beaten to death as if he actually took it, hanging up a body and pretending it was suicide by hanging, or throwing a body into the water and pretending it was suicide by drowning, the slightest mistake may entail most serious consequences. Carefully note the wounds on deceased's body; if these are not on vital places, but the self-strangulation, drowning, or poisoning are apparently bona-fide, then your report may be worded to that effect.

If it is a case of murder by night, and there are no witnesses or the corpse is not forthcoming, it will be necessary to institute secret inquiries after the plaint has been made; it will not do to act upon guesses or to cook up evidence to suit the case and make it complete.

Bribery
In all cases where prosecutor and accused are men of the slightest influence or position, choose experienced and trusty assistants, taking them along with you and never letting them out of your sight even to eat or drink, unless watched by some one, but adjourn the case for a while until they may have finished. Unless you do this, these men will be tampered with, and there will be an end to all justice or redress. This cannot be too cautiously guarded against.

CHAPTER TWO
Miscellaneous Remarks on Wounds

Disease

Whenever an inquest is held over the body of a man who has died from disease, ask first where deceased came from, and then, whether anybody knows him or not, what disease he had, how old he was, and how long ill. If deceased was a slave, inquire for the bill of sale, etc., ask whether he has any relatives, from whom he received medical advice, and what medicine he took. Then proceed to give your verdict in the presence of all parties. If there are no other causes of death, report that the body is of a yellow colour, and nothing but a bag of bones, which could only come about before death; mention also what disease was the cause of death, taking a certificate from the doctor to that effect. If deceased, according to the evidence of all, died of illness and came to his end by no unfair means, no one can apply for a further inquest.

Wherever it is a case of death from illness, the body is emaciated and the colour of the flesh a faded yellow, the mouth and eyes in most cases are shut, the belly sunk in, the two eyes quite yellow, the two hands slightly clenched, the hair in disorder, and perhaps there may be recent or old marks of cauterization upon the body. If no further marks are found upon the corpse, death resulted from disease.

Hunger

If death has happened at the road-side from hunger, the body will be emaciated and of a dull yellow colour, the mouth and eyes shut, the hands slightly clenched, the mouth and teeth of a smoky yellow colour, and the lips will not cover the teeth.

Sudden Death

In cases of sudden death in spring, summer, or the beginning of autumn, there appears after two or three days a slightly livid hue on the lower part of the belly and at the fissures between the ribs. This arises from decomposition after death, the foul matter distributing itself and occupying parts of the skin and flesh; it has nothing to do with the causes of death.

Fright

The corpses of people frightened to death by devils, goblins, etc., will generally be fat and of a slightly yellow hue, the mouth and eyes will be shut, and in the former there will be frothy saliva, but no marks of violence upon the body.

In cases of sudden death the flesh will not have sunk away, in the mouth and nose there will be frothy saliva and the face will be purple and red; this will be the result of the saliva having collected and choked up the windpipe.

Where death has been sudden from fright, etc., the eyes will be open and the pupils white, the mouth will be closed and the teeth firmly set, sometimes the eyes and mouth will be drawn down on one side or the other, from the corners of the mouth and the nostrils there will be a flow of frothy saliva, and the feet and hands will be drawn up.

In cases of death from fright the corpse will be fat and generally of a glossy white, the mouth and eyes closed, with a copious flow of saliva. Sudden death and death by supernatural agency will not be characterized by fatness or the reverse, but the two hands will be clenched, and the nails of the hands and feet will generally be dark blue. Where death has been the result of fright the mouth and eyes will usually be deflected, the hands and feet drawn up, the arms, legs, hands and feet shrunk, and there will be a flow of saliva.

Catching Cold

Where death resulted from catching cold, the whole body will be red and purple, the mouth and eyes open, with a purple liquid oozing out, the lips will be slightly open and the hands not clenched or drawn up.

Where death has resulted from atmospheric causes, the eyes and mouth will be open, the whole body of a yellow colour, with a slight separation of the skin, and both hands and feet stretched out.

Where death has resulted from red eruption there will be small red spots scattered here and there on the body without much swelling.

Heat Apoplexy

Heat apoplexy is generally fatal in the 5th, 6th, and 7th moons; the tongue does not protrude, nor the bowels; the face is white and yellow, and sometimes from the nose, etc., there is a discharge of blood.

Cold

Where a man has been frozen to death, the face will be of a dull yellow, there will be freely saliva in the mouth, the teeth will be hard [closed], the body stiff, and the two arms drawn up on the chest. In washing the body with wine, at the first contact with the hot steam the jaws will become red and the face will become the colour of the *Hibiscuse mutabilis*. Saliva will flow from the mouth, but it will not be sticky.

Hunger

In cases of death from hunger the whole body will be dark-coloured, thin, hard, and rigid. The eyes will be closed, the mouth open, the teeth tightly set, the belly sunk in, and the hands and feet stretched out.

Fright
In cases of death from fright, the eyes will be staring, the mouth open, the two arms stretched out as if in terror.

Repletion
Where death has resulted from over-eating or drinking, begin by making the assistants wash the body with vinegar; then, if there are no wounds, pat the belly with your hand, and if it is swelled up and sounds like a drum, death was caused by repletion, and by the wine penetrating into the heart and lungs. Make the relatives depose as to the amount of wine usually necessary to make deceased drunk, as also to the quantity he took on the present occasion.

Where death has resulted from drinking samshoo, the teeth rattle about and easily drop out, the body is soft, and a watery fluid comes from the mouth and nose. Samshoo should not be heated over the fire in a pewter vessel, or left to stand all night; if thus left for a few days, it may cause death to whoever drinks it, the face turning a dull livid colour.

[Where death has resulted from getting drunk off samshoo, life may be restored by pouring down the throat water collected from the lids of saucepans and cooking-pots.]

Trampled on
Where deceased has been stamped upon and injured internally so as to cause death after over-indulgence in eating and drinking, the appearance of the body will not be a reliable guide. If there were no other causes of death, ejection of food at the mouth, nose, &c., will at any rate be some indication. Make careful inquiries whether deceased had fought with anybody and thus came to be trampled upon before you give your verdict.

Cauterization

In cases of cauterization with a needle, it will be necessary to obtain the certificate of another doctor as to whether death may not have been caused by the operation being performed in a wrong spot. If the five viscera are short of the *yin* (female principle), and acupuncture is performed (from a faulty diagnosis) with a view to add more *yang* (male principle), this is called *chung chieh*. Death is sure to result, the patient dying quietly. The opposite of this is called *ni chileh*, and is equally fatal, but death is not peaceful.

Homo qui sibi ultra modum indulgeat, semine exhausto in ipso feminae corpore moritur. Falso verum diagnoscere perfacile est, hoc erecto, illud dejecto membro. When men and women die of irregularities of the yin and yang, their lips and nails will be of a dull livid colour; in severe cases the whole body will be purple, arising from exhaustion of the latter (vital fluid) or coagulation of the former (blood).

Where death has resulted from an irregularity of the yin, the corpse will be of a dull livid or black colour, resembling a case of poisoning, but of a fainter hue. The mouth and eyes will be shut, the two hands closed, etc.

Bambooing

Where death has resulted from corporal punishment with the bamboo, the marks should be carefully examined as to their breadth, and it should be noted if the scrotum, ribs, waist, or lower abdomen show any subcutaneous appearance of blood.

The smaller bamboo will leave scars 3 in. long by 2 in. on the left, and 3and a half in. long by 3 in. on the right side. Depth, 3 tenths of an inch on either side.

The large bamboo will leave scars from 3 in. to 3 and a half ins. either way on both sides, and three tenths of an inch deep. There will be matter in and around the wounds, and the flesh will be rotten.

It sometimes happens that people die after a bambooing from quite other causes. If the front of the thighs and the lower abdomen is slightly red, do not look on this as a subcutaneous appearance resulting from infliction of the bamboo; for very possibly it came from lying on something hard while being punished, and appeared as might be expected after death. This requires care at the time of examination.

If there are slanting, broken wounds on both sides, several inches long by something less than an inch broad, and reaching down to the bone, with a scab, death resulted from deceased catching cold in wounds inflicted with the bamboo.

Falling from a Height
Where death has resulted from falling down off a tree or house, notice the branches, leaves, etc., the height of the house, the place where deceased's foot slipped, the depth of the mark in the ground, and the particular nature of the wound which caused death. If the injury was internal, blood will flow from the mouth, eyes, ears and nose. If the wound is very severe, be even more careful in your examination, and measure the exact height of the place from which deceased fell.

In cases of falling down either from slipping or tripping, the force being low down, the wounds are consequently on the leg, foot, or arm. Such, whether on the right or left, only injure the limb half way round. If it is a case of being pushed down, then the force, being high up, the wounds will be chiefly on the head and the two wrists. For pushing implies the exertion of force, and the head is the heaviest part of the human body. Thus, if a person was pushed down while he was expecting it, his hands would probably touch the ground first, but, if taken unawares, his head. Although it does not necessarily follow that the wounds are more extensive, they are distinguishable from wounds received in falling down.

Crushed to Death

Where a man has been crushed to death the eyes and tongue will protrude, the hands will be slightly clenched, all over the body there will be traces of dead blood of a dull purple colour; from the nose blood will flow, or a watery fluid; the injured parts will be red and swollen with a subcutaneous appearance of blood; the parts where the skin has been broken will be red and swollen, and perhaps the bones and muscles broken. The above refers to crushing on a vital spot, for if the spot be not vital, death will not ensue; neither will a body which has been crushed after death present these appearances.

Where a man has been crushed to death by a house or wall falling on him, or by a stone, the length and breadth of wounds on the fleshy parts of the body must be reported, and that they were inflicted by something hard; note also if the bones are broken or not. If death was caused by a falling tree, note the size of the wound thus inflicted, which should be oblique and corresponding to the dimensions of the tree. Crushing after death has not the same characteristics.

Where two men are carrying anything on a pole, one strong and the other weak, and the weak one gets crushed, the shoulder as well as the hand and foot on the same side will all be more or less injured. Where the crushing resulted from accidentally rushing up against anything, observe carefully whether the wounds are at the front or on the back, on the right or left side. If on the back, then on the front part of the body there will be traces of injury from knocking against something, and vice versa. So also with regard to the right and left sides.

Choking or Gagging

Wherever death resulted from the forcible stoppage of respiration, the eyes will be open and the eyeballs starting out; from the mouth and nose a watery blood will flow; all over the face there will be a subcutaneous appearance of blood of a dark brown-red colour; the bowels will protrude, etc.

89

Where the mouth and nose have been gagged with clothes or wet paper and death has resulted therefrom, the abdomen will be swelled up and dry.

Whenever a man has been choked by other means, his two hands, the back of his arms either above or below, his heel-bones and chest will all show slight wounds. For to choke a man so that his eyeballs start out requires considerable pressure, and though the body may be kept immovable, the hands and feet must be to a certain extent free. But the hands and feet may have been tied, and it will be necessary to see if there are any such marks.

Held up head downwards
Supposing a man is made drunk and laid down on a carpet or rug, then, when he is sound asleep, rolled up in it and held up head downwards, death will ensue very quickly, but there will be no traces of blood from the mouth and eyes, or, if there are, a little water will soon remove them. There will, however, be a strong exhalation of wine fumes.

Held up head downwards in a tub of water and lime
Sometimes two tubs, such as are frequently covered one over the other and about the height of a man, are used, one being first filled with water in which a quantity of lime is mixed up, and then the victim is thrust in head downwards, the other tub being used to cover him up. Death soon ensues. This is called "going out for a sail." When the body is subsequently washed no wound of any kind will be visible, the face will be yellow and white, as if death had occurred from disease. The flow of blood which might naturally be expected will be arrested by the lime, as also the blood which would have collected and congealed in the face will be similarly dispersed. This can only be substantiated by "bone examination" of the shell of the brain, for the grits of the lime passing through the mouth and nose, which can be washed clean, penetrate right into the brain

90

and may be found sunk in it. From such evidence as this there is no appeal.

Prodding
Where a man has died through being prodded with something hard, there will be a subcutaneous appearance of blood at the back of the ribs, purply red and swollen, three or four inches square or round, the skin not broken. Feel with the hand if any injury has been done to the muscles or bone. This is a non-resisting vital spot.

Trampling of Horses, etc.
Where a man has been trampled to death by a horse, the colour of the body will be slightly yellow, the two arms stretched out, the hair in disorder, blood will flow from the mouth and nose, and the injuries will be of a black colour. Where a vital spot has been trampled upon and death caused thereby, the bones will be broken and the bowels will protrude. If a man is merely knocked down or trampled upon in some non-vital spot, the skin will be broken and the scar will be red and black, but death will not result. The mark of a donkey's hoof is small, and wounds from cow's horns are generally in the pit of the stomach or in the abdomen or ribs. If the skin is not broken, the wound will be red and swollen.

The wounds inflicted by the trampling of men, horses, donkeys and mules are distinguishable by their number and severity. A horse moves with great force, inflicting few wounds but breaking the bones and perhaps forcing out the bowels. Where a prostrate man is trampled upon by a number of horses, the wounds will be many, but not so severe as where a man is knocked down by a horse galloping. If trampled on by men the injuries will be in long-shaped patches, severe at one end and slight at the other. Where many people trample over a man, preventing him from rising, the severity and size of the wounds will vary. The wounds inflicted thus by donkeys and mules are not only smaller than those inflicted by horses, but the halo round the wound is distinctly visible. If a man is gored unawares by an ox, the wound is generally in front on the ribs, lower abdomen, or pit of the stomach. If an ox suddenly rushes at a man so that he has not time to get out of the way, the wound will generally be on the back or ribs.

Crushed
Where a man has been crushed by a cart-wheel, the colour of the corpse will be slightly yellow, the mouth and eyes open, the hands slightly clenched, the hair tightly plaited. [This applies only to instant death.]

Run over
Death generally results from the wheel passing over some vital spot such as the chest or ribs; if the part is not vital, death will not ensue.

A cart may pass over a man either crosswise or lengthwise; crosswise when a man, passing before a cart going too fast to be pulled up, falls down and the cart goes over and kills him. The injury will be either on the neck, head, or chest, back or ribs, and possibly on the arms or legs. If a man is run over by a cart meeting him face to face, the wounds will be on the arms, legs, or ribs, but only on one side, and passing along the body in a straight line. The wounds will be long and generally on the front part of the body. If run over from behind, the wounds will be much the same but on the back.

Lightning
Where a man has been struck by lightning the body will be of a scorched yellow colour, soft and black. The two hands will be partially clenched, the mouth open and the eyes starting out, the hair behind scorched and yellow, and generally in disorder. At the burnt places the skin and flesh will be hard and shrivelled, the clothes on the body burnt to cinders, or perhaps

92

not burnt. The injuries are generally on the head at the back, the sutures open, and the hair looks as if it had been singed off from top to bottom. Occasionally there are patches of loose skin, as large as the hand, of a purply red colour, the flesh is not injured, and on the chest, neck, back, and arms there are streaks like the strokes of the seal character. There are two kinds of death by lightning: one from fright, where no wounds are to be found, the other from being struck where wounds are to be found.

Tigers

Where a man has been bitten to death by a tiger, the colour of the body will be yellow, the mouth and eyes will generally be open, the hands clenched, the hair in confusion, and the wounds torn and uneven. There will be marks also of the animal's tongue and teeth.

Tigers generally bite the head and neck, leaving marks of the claws and feet on the body. The wounds are like holes, in which the bone is sometimes visible. They will be on the chest and legs. There will also be marks of the tiger's claws on the ground, which should be copied by an artist, the head man of the place and the neighbours being present as witnesses. [At the beginning of a month tigers bite the head and neck, in the middle of a month the back and belly, at the end of a month the feet. Cats bite rats in the same way.]

Mad Dogs

Where a man has been bitten by a mad dog and died in consequence, there will be a mark of a wound, and the belly will have swollen up hard. The appearance of the victim in the first stages will be that of a man with a violent cold, terribly afraid of wind, barking every now and then like a dog, wanting to bite people and tear their clothes, the belly pendulous, and micturition difficult.

Snakes, etc.

Where death has been caused by the bite of a snake or reptile, the wound will be black and show marks of the teeth; the parts round it will be livid and swollen, a watery fluid of a yellow colour will flow from the wound, the poison will have penetrated to the extremities, and the body will have swollen up black and shiny.

Rats, etc.

Where a dead body has been gnawed by rats, etc., the skin will be broken, but there will be no appearance of blood, and round the injured parts there will be marks of teeth. Supposing the parts to be ragged and uneven, if inflicted by some other animal, the wound will be on a larger scale.

Directly a case of death on the high-road is reported, proceed at once to examine the body, and observe if there are any wounds, taking a note of the apparent age of deceased, his facial appearance and clothes. If there is any property found with him, make a public delivery of the same to your treasurer, to be kept until identification by his relatives. Buy a coffin and bury the body in a temporary manner, marking the spot with a mark. If it is a case of death by violence your investigations and report must be made with double care.

CHAPTER THREE
Accidental Poisoning

Death is not caused only by such drugs as arsenic or snake-eater but even by gin-seng and the Cyperus esculentus, if constantly taken; the mouth and nose discharging blood, and the skin breaking all over into cracks about an inch apart. In the medical work by the Emperor Huang and his minister Chi, we have mentioned the tendon-swelling, commonly called "the black-rash swelling." A wrong diagnosis will lead to fatal results. All such diseases as also the vulvae morbus are characterized as follows: The nails of the hands and feet are of a dull livid colour, or perhaps quite livid and purple, and in severe cases the head and whole body are both purple, the reason being that the blood has been paralysed and acquires this colour from congelation. In Canton and Fokien they have also miasmatic contagion. If a man is attacked by this let him be pricked at once with the sharp point of a piece of broken crockery-ware, either on the forehead, or between the eyebrows, or on the arms; about a pint of blood taken from him will be enough to effect a cure. If the attack is slight the blood will be red and copious; if severe, purple and scarce. Blood of a blackish purple and very little in quantity indicates that the attack is extremely severe, and recovery next to impossible. The people of those provinces regard a copious flow of blood as a subject of congratulation, and know that when it comes with difficulty recovery is out of the question. The head and face of the corpse are for the most part of a dull livid or entirely purple and black, as also the nails of the hands and feet. On the other hand, there is abscess of the liver and other diseases of the viscera where a foul mass it thrown up, black blood excreted, the rectum swells up, and the bowels protrude: in such cases death must not be hastily attributed to poison. Besides, death is often caused by mixing things which disagree; for instance, you cannot eat honey with onions, nor

95

should there be any dust or cobwebs with a dish of torpedo. If from the rapidity with which death occurs you are led to infer that it was caused by poison, you will fall into grievous mistakes.

Miasmatic contagion is extremely fatal in Yunnan and Canton. The body is not entirely livid, purple, or of a dull black, but the face is of a bright red colour, the lips and mouth purple and black, the chest, abdomen, and throat swelled up, the nails of the hands and feet of a dull livid colour, and from the mouth, eyes, ears, nose, etc., there will be a discharge of blood. If the bones are examined after death, they will be of a cloudy dark-blue colour.

Reptiles

Poison can be taken into the system otherwise than through the stomach, as from the bites of insects, snakes, and such animals, but in such cases there will be the mark of the bite. Where death has ensued from the bite of a mad dog after the wound had healed, there will still be the marks of teeth: note the size of these. All such wounds will be livid and black and swollen.

In cases of death from poisoning the bones will be rotten, and will be found on examination to be of a dull black colour, the chest, pit of the stomach, roots of the teeth, and tips of the fingers, being all of a dark blue colour.

CHAPTER FOUR
Suicide by Poison

Where death has resulted from intentionally taking poison, the mouth and eyes will generally be open, the face of a dull purple or livid colour, the lips purple and black, the nails of the hands and feet of a dull livid, there will be blood from the mouth, eyes, ears, and nose. In severe cases, the whole body will be black and swollen, the face livid and black, the lips curled and blistered, the tongue shrunk up or cracked, rotten, swollen, and slightly protruding. The lips will also be rotten and swollen, sometimes also cracked. The tips of the finger-nails will be black, the throat and belly swollen up, of a black colour and blistered. The body will be marked with livid streaks, the eyes starting out, a purple black blood coming from the ears, mouth, and nose, with the hair on the head and face in disorder.

Before death takes place a foul mass will be thrown up and black blood may be passed. The rectum will be swelled up and the bowels will protrude.

Where poison has been taken death will ensue either at once or at some time in the same day; if the poison is slow, at the expiration of one or two days. The vomiting may be intermittent or continuous. Search carefully deceased's clothes for any remnant of the poison; also the spot where he committed suicide for any pot or vessel that might have contained the drug.

Silver Needle Method to Detect Poison

To detect suicide by poison, take a silver needle, wash it in lye made from the soap bean and insert it into the dead man's mouth, sealing up the mouth tightly with paper. After a little while take it out, and you will find it of a dark blue or black colour, which will not come off if washed again in soap-bean lye. If it is not a case of poison the needle will remain fresh and white.

Another Method

Another method is to take three pints of common rice and boil it soft; then take one pint of good glutinous rice, clean it well, and steam it in a pudding-cloth over the already boiled rice; then take a fowl's egg, a duck's egg will do, make a tiny hole in it and take out the white, throwing it over the glutinous rice and mixing it well up together. Then tie up as before and lay it on top of the boiled common rice, and with three fingers squeeze it up into balls about as big as a hen's egg. Take these quickly, while still hot, and put into the deceased's mouth in front of his teeth, covering up the mouth, ears, eyes, etc., with three or four sheets of paper. Then take several strips of new cotton wool and plunge them into three or four pints of good vinegar, which has been made to boil fast. When they have been some little time immersed, spread grains all over the body and cover over with the cotton wool. If deceased died from the effects of poison, the body will swell up, there will be a foul and stinking discharge from the mouth, blown out upon the cotton wool. [You had better not stand too near.] Afterwards take away the cotton wool and the glutinous rice, when, if it has been turned black and foul smelling by the discharge, you may return a verdict of death by poison. The absence of these signs must be regarded as proving that death was not caused in this way.

Fowl Method

Another method is to thrust a lump of boiled rice into deceased's throat and allow it to remain there a little while, the mouth being meanwhile covered up with a sheet of paper. Then take it out and give it to a fowl to eat. If the fowl dies, poison is present.

98

Full or Empty Stomach

If poison is taken on a full stomach, the abdomen will swell and be of a livid colour, but the lips and finger-nails will not be livid; if taken on an empty stomach, the results are exactly reversed. Where, however, poison is taken by a man with a weak stomach or by an invalid of long standing, and death occurs directly, neither the abdomen, mouth, lips, or finger nails will necessarily be livid. The disease under which deceased may have been suffering will require to be taken into consideration.

Where Time has Elapsed

Where some time has elapsed since the poison was swallowed, and it is no longer possible to detect its presence, first take a silver needle and thrust it into deceased's throat; then, beginning from the feet upwards, plaster over the body with hot grains and vinegar, allowing a free passage through the mouth for the air inside the body. If a poisonous vapour is emitted the needle will turn to a black colour. If the poultice of grains and vinegar is applied from the head downwards, the poison vapour will be forced the other way and can only be detected by applying the silver needle to the rectum.

Where other food has been taken on the top of poison, and it becomes impossible to detect the presence of the latter, the ordinary operation by the mouth may be performed by the latter method.

Whether Administered Before or After Death

Where poison was accidentally or intentionally taken by any one, the whole body will be of a livid colour, retaining the skin and flesh for many days; or it may be of a black colour. After some time the skin and flesh will rot and fall off, leaving the bones exposed and of a dull black colour. The chest, pit of the stomach, roots of the teeth, and tips of the fingers will be of a dark blue or livid hue.

Where poison has been administered to a dead man in order to pass off his death as the result thereof, the skin, flesh and bones will be of a yellow colour.

Care must be taken not to confuse the accidental with the intentional taking of poison.

Swallowing Snakes

A case is recorded of a man who tied his victim's hands and feet, and forced into his mouth the head of a snake, applying fire at the same time to its tail. The snake jumped down the man's throat and passed into his stomach, but at an inquest held over the body no traces of wounds were found to which death might be attributed. This, however, may be detected by examination of the bones, which, from the head downwards, will be found entirely of a bright red colour, caused by the dispersion of the blood; and, moreover, the more the bones are scraped away the more bright coloured do they become.

CHAPTER FIVE
All Kinds of Poisons

Ku

Where Ku poison has been taken, the whole body, head, face, and breast, will be of a dark blue or black colour. The body will swell, and there will be a discharge of blood from the mouth and anus.

To Make Ku

Ku is made as follows: Take a quantity of insects of all kinds and throw them into a vessel of some kind, and let a year pass away before you look at them again. The insects will have killed and eaten each other until there is only one survivor, and this one is Ku. The word is derived from *ch'ung*, insects, and *min*, a vessel, etc.

Where death has resulted from gold worm *ku*, the body will be thin and emaciated, and of a yellow and white colour, the eyes will have sunk in, the teeth will be visible, the lips will be shrunk, the abdomen will have sunk in, and a needle will show a shaded yellow stain, which will not come off when washed in soap-bean lye.

Sometimes the body swells and the skin and flesh look as if scalded into blisters by hot water, with here and there traces of matter, and the tongue, lips and nose cracked and broken. These are unmistakable signs of gold worm *ku.* The first paragraph applies to thin people, this latter to fat ones.

Both in Kiangnan and Kiangsi there is a kind of poison called *Illicium religiosum*, very much resembling ku in its action, only the lips are more cracked, the gums livid and black; it operates after twenty-four hours, blood flowing from the nine apertures.

Where croton seeds have been taken the mouth will be dry, the two cheeks red, the top of the head, palms of the hands and soles of the feet will be hot; there will be incessant purging.

Arsenic

When sublimed arsenic has been taken, in a little while the whole body will be covered with small blisters, and turn to a livid or black colour, the eyes will start out, and on the tongue there will be little broken blisters, besides which the mouth and lips will be cracked, the two eyes will swell out, the belly will swell, the rectum will swell and gape, and the finger-nails will be livid and black.

Swallowing sublimed arsenic will be attended with vomiting and painful griping, delirium, and discharges of blood from the seven apertures of the head; the mouth and lips will also be livid and black. If taken on a full stomach, the upper half of the body will be livid; on an empty stomach, the lower half. *Testes magnopere crescent.*

Where *Corydalis heterocarpa* poison has been taken, blood will flow from every aperture on the body; its characteristics will be like those of sublimed arsenic.

Ice-flakes (Borneo Camphor)

A little more than a mace of Borneo camphor taken in hot wine will be enough to stop respiration, make the blood boil and flow from the seven apertures.

Quicksilver

Death from swallowing quicksilver may be detected by gold which will be turned white.

Where a man has been poisoned by vegetable or mineral substances, the body will be marked here and there with swellings like blows from the fist, or large patches of a livid or dark colour. The nails will be black, the flesh on the body cracked and slightly bloody; the belly may be swollen, accompanied by haemorrhage from the rectum.

102

Wine
Where a man has been poisoned with wine, the belly will
swell, accompanied by haemorrhage from the rectum.

Poisonous Mushrooms
Where death has resulted from eating poisonous mushrooms,
the nails of the hands and feet as well as the whole body will be
of a livid or black colour, much blood will come from the
mouth and nose, the skin and flesh will be cracked all over, the
tongue and bowels will protrude.

Dross of Silver
No mention is made in any book of the means of detecting the
presence of the dross of silver used as a poison.

Salts
Where death has been caused by taking salts, the hair will be in
disorder, the nails off, and on the chest there will be marks of
nails in the flesh, for the pain will be so acute that the victim
will roll about on the ground and tear himself to pieces.

Where salts have been taken, blisters will not rise on
the body, the mouth will not be cracked, the belly will not
swell, the nails will not be livid, the needle will not turn black,
but will be of a slightly dull colour and will come white with
washing, the whole body will be yellow, the two eyes closed,
and in the mouth there may be some frothy saliva. Although
the body decomposes, the heart and lungs will not. If some of
the liquid [in the stomach] be heated over a fire it will become
salt.

Soda
Death is sometimes caused by a dose of washing-soda, given to
a sick man in his medicine. In such cases the hair is in disorder,

the finger-nails torn off, the body bent up, and blood flows from the nose and mouth.

Ficus Japonica
Where Ficus japonica has been taken, the victim gets confused as if he had had a paralytic stroke, or as if delirious.

Bitter Almonds
Bitter almonds are poison; they are found in all the north-western provinces. Taken either raw or cooked they are not hurtful, but a good many eaten half-cooked will cause death. The eyes of the body will be closed, the tongue, lips, ears, fingers and toes will be livid, and the belly will be swollen with patches of a livid colour on it. [To cure a patient, make him sick.]

Aconite
Aconite is poison. It is found on the left of the Yangtze. Its juice, when boiled, is called *she wang*, and is much stronger: if spread on wounds it will cause death instantly.

CHAPTER SIX
Extraordinary Poisons

Hsien and Tortoise Flesh
Spinach eaten with tortoise is poison. [This is a plant with a long, reddish stalk; the tortoise alluded to has three feet and hears with its eyes.]

Monstrosities and Unnatural Food.
Monstrosities in birds, beasts, reptiles and fishes are the result of the parents having experienced some disturbing influence. Such, for instance, are animals with two tails, crabs with one claw, sheep with one horn, and fowls with four legs. Similarly, there are irregular creations, such as white birds with black heads, black fowls with white heads, white horses with dark feet and the reverse. Some animals are not extraordinary in their appearance, but their flesh has unusual characteristics; for instance, if let fall to the ground dust will not adhere to it; hung up all night it will still be warm in the morning; no sun or fire-heat will dry it, and put into water it will move. Sometimes it is the viscera only, and not the skin and flesh which exhibit these peculiarities. For instance, the liver is of a dull dark-blue colour, the kidneys purple and black. Fishes without entrails and gall-bladder, oxen with only one "leaf" of the liver belong to the same class.

Occasionally something which is generally found to agree with the stomach very well, taken with another particular kind of food, becomes extremely hurtful; as for instance, shell-fish eaten with venison is poison, mutton with minced-meat cream is unwholesome, sheep's liver with red pepper causes purging, pork eaten with carum destroys the navel. There are also some kinds of food which do not ordinarily affect each other but when taken into the stomach become living things; as for instance, raw minced carp, eaten with butter produces

105

maggots, tortoise-flesh eaten with spinach produces tortoises [see ante], beef eaten with pork produces small white worms about an inch long, as also does pork and mutton eaten with boiled or broiled sticks of the mulberry or *Broussonetia papyrifera.*

[Cases are given of death resulting from drinking pond-water which had been poisoned by snakes, water in which flowers had stood, eating the flesh of a fowl which had swallowed a centipede, drinking tea or water which had been standing uncovered all night, wearing clothes which had been wetted with perspiration and dried in the sun, going into rooms, etc., which had long been shut up.]

Asphyxiation
Death from asphyxiation is caused by the leaking of the stove-bed. The corpse is soft and without marks; death is painless as if the result of nightmare.

BOOK FOUR

CHAPTER ONE
Methods of Restoring Life

Hanging

Where a man has been hanging from morning to night, even though already cold, life may be restored; if from night to morning, the operation will be more difficult. If there is warmth beneath the heart, life may be restored after the body has hung more than a day. On no account cut the rope, but gently taking the body in your arms, have the knot untied and lay the body out at full length. Then let someone place his feet on the shoulders of the patient and firmly hold up the head by its hair, not allowing it to hang down for a moment. Let another manipulate the throat, another rub the chest, and another chafe the feet and hands, pulling them backwards and forwards. If the body is already stiff, let them be gradually bent at the joint. If this is done, in about the space of a meal respiration will begin, and with the recommencement of breathing the eyes will open. When consciousness is restored, give the patient some cinnamon tea and some gruel to drink in order to keep his throat moist, and let two men blow into his ears through small tubes. Recovery under these conditions is certain.

Another method.: Stop up the patient's mouth tightly with your hand, and in a little over four hours respiration will be restored.

Another method: Take equal parts of soap bean and *Anemone hepatica* finely powdered, and blow a quantity of this, about as much as a bean, into the patient's nostrils.

Another method: Take two or three tenths of an ounce of genuine goat's blood, rub it down very smooth and mix it with good wine. A dose of this will cause instant recovery.

Another method: In all cases where men or women have

107

been hanged, a recovery may be effected even if the body has become stiff. You must not cut the body down, but, supporting it, untie the rope and lay it down in some smooth place on its back, with the head propped up straight. Bend the arms and legs gently, wrap up the pudenda, etc., in cotton wool that no air may escape, and let someone sitting behind the head with his feet on the shoulders pull the patient's hair tightly. Pull the arms out straight, let there be a free passage through the wind-pipe, and let two people blow incessantly into either ear through a bamboo tube or a reed, rubbing the chest all the time with the hand. Take the blood from a live fowl's comb and drop it into the throat and nostrils (the left nostril of a woman, the right of a man; also using a cock's comb for a man, a hen's for a woman). Re-animation will be immediately effected. If animation has been suspended for a long time, there must be plenty of blowing and rubbing; do not think that because the body is cold all is necessarily over.

Drowning
Where a man has been in the water a whole night, recovery may still be effected. Pound some soap bean, wrap it up in cotton, and insert it into the rectum; in a little while the water will be discharged and life restored. Or, having bent the patient's legs, let him be carried by the feet over another man's shoulders, back to back, when he will vomit forth the water and be revived.

Another method: Break up part of a mud wall and pound it to dust; lay the patient thereon on his back, and cover him up with the same excepting only his mouth and eyes. Thus, the water will be absorbed by the mud and a recovery will be effected. This method is a very sure one even though the body has become stiff.

Another method: Sprinkle the face all over, excepting only the mouth and nose, with hot sand, replacing it as it gets cold or damp. After several changes of sand, animation will be restored.

Another method: Pour half a cupful of vinegar into the nostrils. Wrap up some lime in cotton, and insert it into the anus. Water will be discharged and re-animation will follow.
Hold the patient up by his feet and pour good wine into the nostrils and anus.

Another method: Hold the patient up by his feet, strip off his clothes, clean out the navel, and let two men blow into his ears through bamboo tubes.

Another method: Strip off the patient's clothes without loss of time, and cauterize him on the navel.

Another method: Immediately on taking a man out of the water, prise open his mouth and insert something to keep the teeth apart that the water may come out; blow through tubes into both his ears; take some finely powdered *Finellia tuberifera* and blow it into his nose; and fill a tube with powdered soap bean and blow it into his anus. If the accident happens during summer, take the drowned man and lay him crosswise on his belly over a cow's back, two people supporting his head and feet; then let the cow be walked about quietly, when the water in the stomach will be thrown up and pass away also through the penis and anus. Give the patient green-ginger tea and decoction of rose maloes or the juice of raw ginger. If a cow is not to be had, let someone go down on his hands and knees and lay the drowned man across his back as before; then let the man on his hands and knees wriggle himself about when the water will come out. If it is impossible to get a cow and no one is willing to undertake the job, a large pot or jar will answer the purpose. If it is in winter strip off the wet clothes and change them; heat some salt, wrap it up in a cloth and apply it to the navel; spread out a mattress and bedding and cover it over with plenty of ashes from reeds, grass, etc.; then lay the drowned man on it face downwards, placing a small pillow under the navel, and sprinkle ashes thickly all over the body, covering it with bedding, etc., and

109

taking care that none of the ash gets into the patient's eyes; pour into the mouth, kept open as mentioned above, rose maloes and green-ginger tea, blowing into the ears, nose, and anus as for the summer method. In winter, when consciousness is restored, give the patient a little hot wine to drink; in summer, a little gruel. The power of ashes to absorb water in this way may be tested on drowned flies, which, if covered up with ashes, will revive.

Another method: Take a small wine-jar and throw into it a strip of lighted paper, turn it upside down and place the mouth of the jar *in umbilico*; when the jar is cold repeat the process until the water comes out, which will be a sign of recovery.

Another method: If when the body is first recovered there is the slightest sign of breathing or the least warmth on the chest, make some one quickly take off his underclothing, and, having wrapped the drowned man in them, lay the body across his own and roll it gently backwards and forwards so that the water may come out of the stomach. If the water comes out there is a good chance of recovery. Also burn some thick paper under his nose for a little while and then blow some finely-powdered soap bean into his nostrils. If there is the slightest sneeze a recovery can be effected.

Wounds
In cases of knife-wounds, etc., where the membrane has not been pierced, take about as much as a soap bean of olibanum and myrrh, mash up smooth, mix with half a cup of urine and half a cup of good wine, and heat altogether; when warm, administer a draught. Also take dolomite powder, or cuttle-fish bones, or dragon's bones, and bind over the mouth of the wound; the bleeding will thus be stopped. Two cases of examination by an assistant Prefect Chuan Ting are on record where the wounded men not being quite dead, he made the head man take the heart of an onion, heat it very hot and apply

110

it to the wound; the result was a sudden inhalation of air. A second application of onion causes no pain.

Dolomite powder (so-called) contains olibanum, myrrh, archangelica, lophanthus, aconite, *Magnolia hypoleuca*, iris, *Anemone hepatica*, laka wood, Aralia edulis, calomel, sapan-wood, sandal-wood, dragon's bones, musk, and dolomite.

Another Method: Where a knife-wound keeps on bleeding, take some laka wood, scrape it with a piece of broken crockery-ware, rub it fine with a stone and spread it on the wound. The bleeding will stop and there will be no scar.

Pain Killer
Where the pain of a knife-wound etc., continues, take some good "chicken-bone" charcoal, which rings when thrown on the ground, and knead it up into a lump with an equal quantity of clear resin; then take plenty of the expressed juice of old leeks, mix and let it dry of itself (not in the sun) repeating several times, when nothing but a fine dust will remain. (The mixture should have been previously prepared on the 3rd of the 3rd moon, 5th of the 5th, or 7th of the 7th.) If spread on the wounded part the pain will cease at once, and when well the flesh will appear as usual.

Knife Wounds and Bowels Protruding
Where a wound has been inflicted with metal and the bowels protrude, take five pints of rye and nine pints of water, boil away to four pints, strain it clear, wait till it is quite cold, make the wounded man lie down on a mat, and let someone squirt the liquid from his mouth over the patient's back; the bowels will gradually recede. The liquid must be squirted unknown to the patient, and there must not be a lot of people talking in the room at the time. If the bowels do not recede, take the mat by the four corners, raise it up and gently shake it; the bowels will then go in. When in, sew up the wound tightly with thread dipped in hempseed oil, binding the body round with silk

111

moistened in the same way. Be careful not to shake the patient about and thus reopen the wound.

Arrow-heads
Where a wound has been inflicted by the head of an arrow, take some meat which has been a long time salted, peel off the skin, a good red piece should be chosen, and chop up the fat very fine until it is pulpy, mix with it some ground ivory and human fingernails until the ingredients are well distributed, and apply a thick lump of this to the place where the arrow-head is; in about the time it takes to eat a meal the arrow head will come out.

Scalding
In cases of injury from scalding, get a large oyster and put it in a basin with its mouth upwards somewhere quite away from people; wait till its shell opens and then shake in from a spoon an equal portion of genuine musk. The oyster will then close its shell and its flesh will be melted into a liquid. Add a little more of the above ingredients, and with a fowl's feather brush it over the parts and round and round the wound, getting nearer and nearer every time, until at last you brush it into the wound: the pain will gradually cease. A small oyster will do if a big one is not to be had. This is a first-rate prescription. When the burning has stopped, take the shell of the oyster just used, burn it to a cinder, but so that it keeps its properties, pound it to dust, and mix with it a little Borneo camphor and musk, and apply it round the wound. If it is a place where there are no oysters, Borneo camphor alone rubbed round and round the wound and finally into it will heal the place gradually.

Cold Water
In cases of scalding, on no account apply cold water, cold things, mud from the bottom of wells, etc., to the injured parts, for the heat will thus be driven farther in, and the least result

will be that the parts will contract, though if the poison of the heat extends as far as the heart, death will speedily ensue.

To Cure Scalds
Take good Hangchow meal ground very fine, and mix it with good hair-oil and spread it on the parts. If hair-oil is not to be had, pine-oil will do as well.

Another Method: Spread over the wound a quantity of very old soy. When cured there will be a black scar.

Another Method: Take some Lui Chi Nu (a plant named after its discoverer) pounded fine, and having first brushed over the wound with a fowl's feather dipped in glutinous rice water, sprinkle it upon the wound. The pain will cease and there will be no scar. Generally speaking, it is advisable in the case of a scald to begin by sprinkling the wound with powdered salt in order to preserve the flesh, and then to apply remedies.

Another Method: Rhubarb mixed with rice-vinegar will effect a cure in two days.

Sunstroke, Heat Apoplexy
Where a man has received a *coup de soleil*, quickly dig a hole in the ground and pour in some water; mix the water up with the mud and give it to him to drink; he will then recover.

If cold water is given in such cases, death will be the result. Cover over the patient with warm ashes taken out of a stove, and apply a cloth which has been dipped in hot water to the abdomen, ribs, etc. After some time consciousness will be restored. On no account give anything cold to eat.

Where a man falls down overpowered by the heat, carry him into a shady and cool spot; give no cold water to drink, but apply a cloth or something dipped in hot water to the lower part of the abdomen, letting a constant supply of hot water drip upon the cloth, so that the heat penetrates to the bowels. If warmth is induced the patient will gradually come round. Should there be no hot water ready to hand, scoop up some of the hot earth from the roadside and pile it up on the abdomen, the more the better, changing it as it gets cold, and afterwards giving cooling medicines. Or, if hot water cannot be had, pile up hot earth as before, and having made a hole in the middle of it, *jube circumstantes in hoc mingere*, and thus effect a cure.

Where a man is quite stupid from the effects of heat, let him chew a good-sized piece of garlic and wash it down with some cold water. If he is unable to chew it, mash it up with a little water and give it him to drink; consciousness will be restored at once. Suppose a case of a thirsty man not being able to procure water to drink; let him chew up a piece of raw garlic about two inches in length, and salivating it well, swallow it. This will be equivalent to a quart of water.

In cases of heat apoplexy, roast a pint of hemp-seed black, spread it out till cold, pound it up, and administer mixed with fresh-drawn water.

Freezing to Death
In cases of death from cold, the arms and legs are stiff, the jaws close set. If there is the slightest sign of respiration, heat some ashes in a large pot, wrap them up and apply to the heart, changing when cold. When the eyes open, give warm wine and thin gruel in small quantities at a time. If the patient is brought near the fire before warmth has been communicated to the heart, the conflicting sensations of heat and cold will cause death.

Another method: Take a piece of carpet or mat, wrap the body up and secure it by a string, lay it down on a level spot; and let two people, standing on either side, roll it backwards and forwards from one to the other with their feet. When the arms and legs are warm consciousness will be restored.

114

Laughter

Where a man has fallen into the water in winter and has quite lost all consciousness from cold, if there is the slightest warmth about the chest, life may still be restored. Should the patient show the least inclination to laugh, stop up his nose and mouth at once, or he will soon be unable to stop laughing and it will be impossible to save him. On no account bring the patient hastily to the fire, for the sight of the fire will excite him to immoderate laughter and a recovery will be impossible.

Where a frozen person has been restored to consciousness, administer green ginger pounded up with the skin and old orange-peel also pounded up, the two being mixed with three pints of water and boiled down to one.

Nightmare

In cases of nightmare, do not at once bring a light, or going near call out hastily to the person, but bite his heel or big toe and gently utter his name. Also spit on his face and give him ginger tea to drink; he will then recover.

In cases of nightmare where the patient cannot be waked, change his position a little and quietly utter his name; he will then awake. If there was a light burning at the time keep it alight; otherwise do not kindle one.

Another method: Blow into the patient's ears through small tubes, pull out fourteen hairs from his head, make them into a twist and thrust into his nose. Also give salt and water to drink.

Another method: Express half a cup of the juice of leeks and pour into the nostrils. In winter use the root, which will also cause sneezing.

Another method: Cauterize the two great toes on the spot where the hair grows.

Another method: Powdered soap bean, about as much as one bean, may be blown into the nostrils. A sneeze may give a free passage for air, and will even effect a recovery after three or four days.

In cases of nightmare, where the body is not quite cold, administer rose maloes, mixed with wine; a recovery will thus be effected.

Goblins

Where death resulted from seeing goblins etc., or an invalid has gone off suddenly in his sleep, the categorical denomination is the same. Take the heart of a leek and thrust it up the nostrils (the left of a man, the right of a woman), about six or seven inches; cause the eyes to open and the blood to flow, and life will be restored.

Look along the inner edge of the upper lips for blisters like grains of Indian corn and prick them with a needle.

Take powdered soap bean or raw *Pinellia tutberifera* and blow about as much as a bean into the nostrils.

Fumigate the nostrils with the smoke of burnt sheep-dung.

Steep some cotton-wool in half a cup of good vinegar and squeeze it into the patient's nose. Grasp his two hands; do not let him be frightened, and in a little he will recover.

Cauterize him on the navel, blow powdered soap bean into his nose, or pour the juice of leeks into his ears.

Express the juice of raw *Acorus terrestris* and give the patient a cupful to drink.

Death from Fright

Where a man has been frightened into a fit, administer one or two cups of warm wine when he will recover.

Falls and Blows

In cases of the five deaths (child-birth, fright, strangulation, nightmare and drowning) or death from falls or blows, if the heart is only a little warm a recovery may be effected even though a day has elapsed. Place the dead man on the ground in

116

squatting posture, like a Buddhist priest: let somebody pull his hair down towards the ground (i.e., in order to get the nostrils into a horizontal position), and blow through a bamboo or paper tube a quantity of raw *Pinellia tutberifera* in powder into the nose. If consciousness returns, administer pure juice of raw ginger to counteract the poison of the *Pinellia tuberifera*.

In cases of sudden death from falling from a height, tumbling down, nightmare, etc., if the body is not cold, mix some rose maloes with wine and give it to the patient to drink. If he swallows it, he will live.

Death from Falling and being Crushed
Where a man has fallen and been severely crushed, blood will flow from the mouth and ears, and unconsciousness will ensue. If there are any signs of vitality or the body is at all soft, a recovery may be effected. But the patient should not be surrounded by a crowd of excited people, as this will prevent him from recovering himself; a relative should speak to him, support him, and place him in a sitting position on the ground. His arms and legs should be then bent up close to his body, and after a little he should be placed in the lap of the person who spoke to him, *ano ejus genu obstructo ne flatus effugiat*. If there is the slightest return to consciousness, let him be removed to the place where he generally sleeps, and let the doors and windows be closed up tightly to darken the room. Then, having again bent his arms and legs, he should be placed again in the same position and not allowed to lie down. Warm urine of a child should be then administered; horse's urine is the best, but if not procurable a man's will do, rejecting the beginning and end of the discharge, and taking care that it is clear and flows quickly, and not that of anyone who has eaten onions or garlic. Give one or two cupfuls of it; if it gets down his throat a recovery will be effected. Also, give "four ingredient" broth, three times the original prescription, putting in peach kernel, without the skin and with the point taken off,

117

and safflower, each one ounce, *Aralia edulis* and southern *Crataeguts cuneata*, pounded up, each two ounces, raw rhubarb two ounces, a bowl of child's urine, and if in summer add about a twentieth of an ounce of gentian

Aralia edulis ... ...1 mace.
Hsiung from Ssuch'uana (blood purifier)... ... 7 cenid.
Rehmannia qlutinosa ... ...3 mace.
Cooked paeonia albiflora ... ...3 mace.

Take plenty of quick running water, and warm up the above prescription over a quick fire, pour it into a bowl and hold under the wounded man's nose, so that the steam may penetrate into the bowels, and the sickness be avoided which would follow if taken at once in the mouth. Give a small cupful as a dose, administering another at a short interval if not retained. Keep on giving doses until all is gone, not permitting the patient to lie down. When the medicine has been taken, the anus must be kept still more tightly closed so as to prevent the passage of wind. If the medicine has already begun to operate and the anus be not tightly closed, a recovery will be impossible, for the air (necessary to life) will all escape from behind. Wait until you can hear that the medicine has begun to operate and there have been several internal heavings, then delay no longer. but support the patient that the discharge may take place. This discharge will be entirely of a purple colour. When half the poison has been got rid of, the patient may sleep. If the discharge is all faecal matter, stop giving the medicine if not, one or two more doses will do no harm. Subsequently, the patient will be gradually restored to strength; medicines for this purpose must not be incautiously administered.

Snake and Reptile Bites
Poisonous snakes can destroy life, but the danger may be averted by cutting out the wound with a sharp knife.

In cases of snake or reptile bites where no medicine is procurable at the moment, take a cupful of the juice of the indigo-plant, half of an ounce of powdered orpiment, mix and spread on the wound, administering the liquid part as a draught. If no indigo plant is to be had, use prepared indigo or indigo dye.

If a man is bitten by the *hui fu* or large-headed snake and the poison penetrates, he will die. Quickly take some cord and bind tightly round the wounded part, so as to prevent the poison from reaching the heart and bowels. Let someone take a mouthful of rice and vinegar or wine, apply his mouth to the wound and suck out the poison, spitting it out and changing the wine or vinegar. Let him continue until the wound is a light-coloured red and the swelling has gone down, taking care not to swallow the poison. Another method is to drink some hemp-seed oil to counteract the effect of the poison on the heart and to spread powdered ginger on the wound.

Where death has resulted from the bite of a snake, take some scented iris and mix it with a decoction of *Ophiopogon japonicus* and administer a dose. If in a hurry use water instead; life will be thus restored.

Another method: Take 1 oz. of magpie's dung, half an ounce of orpiment, mix with wine and administer as a draught, one third of an ounce at a time. Smear the liquid over the wound.

Mad Dog Bites
Before the poison has had time to disseminate, take seven cantharides (*Mylablus cichorii*), pull off their heads, feet, and wings, and boil them with two hen's eggs; take out the insects and eat the eggs without salt, etc. Clots of blood will then appear in the urine. If the penis swells up and is painful, it is because the clots of blood have not entirely passed away. Another dose will clear thein out and the pain will cease.

Another method: Fry some of these insects with rice, wait till the rice is shrivelled and yellow, take out the insects, pound the rice to powder, boil an egg, and eat as in the former

119

prescription. When the blood clots have all passed away, recovery will ensue.

Another method: On being bitten, go at once to a pond or river and wash the wound thoroughly, squeezing out the blood and drinking plenty of the juice of raw ginger. The poison may be thus counteracted. Close up the wound tightly with bandages so that the air may not get to it.

The Seven Scruple Powder

Good red oxide ... ... 1 mace 2 cand. (weight)

Genuine musk ... ... I cand. 21i.

Borneo camphor .... 1 cand 2 li

Olibanum ... ...1 mace 5 cand

Safflower....... ... ... 1 mace 5 cand

Myrrh ... ...1 mace 5 cand

Dragon's blood ... .1 ounce

Catechu ... ...2 mace 4 cand.

Procure the above drugs, choosing such as are brought from places most noted for producing them, and at noon on the 5th day of the 5th moon, mix them all up into a fine powder, stow them away in an earthenware jar, and seal the top with wax; the longer kept the better. No more than seven scruples should be taken as a dose, and must not be taken during pregnancy.

The above prescription is especially adapted for curing wounds inflicted by metal weapons: wounds from falls, blows, etc., where the bones or muscles are broken. Where the flow of blood cannot be stopped, take the seven scruple powder, mix with wine and administer as a draught; then take a similar preparation and spread it on the wound. If it is a severe wound from some sharp weapon, or the gullet severed, do not bind it up with a fowl's skin, but sprinkle the above powder all over it; the pain and the blood will stop, and favourable symptoms will appeal. The same prescription may also be used for a number of poisons which have no specific name, mixed and

120

administered as above. Wounds from blows yield infallibly to this treatment.

In cases where coroners, in examining wounds, happen to have no medicines with. them, or in out of the way places where there is no good doctor, and it is to be feared that slight wounds may become severe ones, that severe ones may result in death, this prescription is invaluable on account of its infallibility. If reverently preserved and produced as occasions require, the aggravation of slight wounds may be avoided, and the fatal effects of severe ones turned aside; not one life, but two may be saved (including that of accused), a benevolent act indeed. Moreover, it is cheap and easy for anybody to make, therefore the prescription is given that benevolent people may avail themselves of it.

Another prescription much used in Szechuan: Old cash, half oz. boiled in vinegar; Peroxide of iron, as the preceding; Dragon's blood (from the tail); Olibanum; Myrrh; Catechu. The ingredients, which should be all finely powdered, may be used for healing wounds from blows or falling. The prescription has often been tested with the most astonishing results. The powder should be mixed with wine and enough taken to cause intoxication. When the wounds are healed it will be necessary *a coitu centum dies abstinere.*

CHAPTER TWO
Antidotes Against Various Poisons
Where arsenic has been taken but a little time, beat up from ten to twenty eggs in a bowl, throw in three mace of powdered alum and administer as a draught. After the vomiting give another dose, and when all has been thrown up a recovery will be effected. Where the arsenic has been some time swallowed and has already passed into the bowels so that it cannot be thrown up, take a lump of lead 4 oz. in weight and rub it on a stone with well water, administering the black liquid which results as fast as it is made; when it is all rubbed away favourable symptoms will appear. After the vomiting mentioned in the first method administer a dose of this lead and water so as entirely to counteract the poison and prevent any further pain.

Another method: Where arsenic has been swallowed quickly administer a dose of hot duck's blood; the poison will thus be neutralized. Or give a dose of clear manure, which will have the same effect.

Another method: Boil some bean-curd into a thick liquid and drink it, or mix the juice of liquorice with an infusion of indigo and drink it, or drink the whey of boiled bean-curd.

Croton Oil
Where croton oil has been taken and the purging cannot be stopped, boil a pint of large beans and drink the juice.

Rhubarb, gentian, the shoots of phragmites, fungi, and *Veratrum nigrum* will stop purging caused by croton seeds.

The juice of plaintain leaves pounded up will also effect-the same result.

The juice of black beans is an antidote to *Illicium religiosum*. Or, take an old calyx of a water-lily with the stem attached and let it dry, bite it off and boil in two or three cupfuls of water;

122

administer this as a draught. If not procurable, use the heart of the nelumbium or a joint of the arrowroot plant, boil in water and administer the liquid nearly cold. The poison will thus be dispersed.

For Ficus japonica drink some juice of blue cerulean or liquorice-root. Medicines are dangerous in such cases.

Bitter Almonds
Drink a decoction of the bark of the apricot tree, and life may be restored even though at the last gasp.

For cantharides, take some pig's lard and bean-juice, crystallized salt and infusion of indigo, and administer as a draught. Or take some salt water, boil in it pig's lard and croton oil, or the juice of black beans, and give as a dose. Or administer a draught of soapy water and tickle the throat afterwards with a goose quill. Vomiting will ensure recovery.

Another method is to give half a dozen raw fowl's or duck's eggs; if sickness can be caused a recovery will be effected. In case the teeth are tightly set they may be forced open with a chop-stick.

Mushrooms
Fungi are very common at Ningpo and in the neighbourhood, differing from one another in species. Some are fatally poisonous, being impregnated with the venom of snakes and reptiles. A Buddhist priest recommends the following method: Make a hole in the ground, fill it with water, and stir it up till quite thick with mud; wait a little while, and then administer a draught of this, which will effect a recovery. This prescription is mentioned in the Chinese Herbal. The mushrooms which grow on the sycamore tree, if eaten, cause uncontrollable laughter, and are commonly called the "laughing mushrooms." The above remedy is important to people who live among the hills.

Where Corydalis heterocarpa has been taken, a dose of the juice of excrement will effect a cure; or supposing the poisonous water has been swallowed in which some may have been steeped, and that there is a discharge of blood from every possible outlet, then quickly take an egg which has been sat upon for some time, mash it up fine, and administer it mixed up with hempseed oil. If the poison is vomited a recovery may be effected.

When enough fungus has been taken to cause vomiting, chewing fresh leaves of the honeysuckle will be found to be an efficient remedy.

Aconite
A remedy for aconite is rice-sugar and black-beans mixed with cold water.

For decoction of aconite, the juice of sweet-grass, or the leaves of the small bean, duck-weed, and *Platycodon grandiflorum* mixed with cold water.

Calomel
For calomel, take 5 lb. of pewter and make a pot. Put into it 15 lb. of spirit, I lb. of smilax and 3 mace of resin; seal up the pot hermetically and boil it for twenty-four hours in water; bury it in the ground that the fire-poison may be absorbed, and drink every morning and evening several cups. The urine should be received in an earthen vessel, and will show a sediment. The medicine should be continued until the muscles and bones are no longer sore. A draught of fresh water will counteract the effects of Borneo camphor.

Where salts have been taken administer a draught of the water in which a duster has been boiled (i.e. the dirty rag used by Chinese to clean their tables, etc.). If sickness can be produced the patient may recover.

Swallowing Gold
In cases of poisoning from swallowing gold, the flesh of the partridge should be eaten; for silver, gentian and liquorice-root. Salt used to wash gold, and the fat of camels, donkeys and horses, as also *Spondias amara*, will all be found to soften gold; sheep's fat will act similarly upon silver. If gold or silver has been swallowed, administer the above remedies according to circumstances; the metal will thus be softened and be easily passed.

General
As a general remedy for all poisons, the *Ku* poison (see ante) and all kinds of mineral poisons, rub down stone crabs with hot water and administer as a draught.

Quicksilver in the Ear
Where quicksilver has got into the ear, lay a piece of gold under the ear as a pillow; the quicksilver will then come out of itself. If quicksilver has got into the flesh and has contracted the muscles, iron the parts over with a piece of gold; the quicksilver will then come out attracted by the gold and a recovery will be effected.

Asphyxiation
In cases of asphyxiation a draught of cold water will bring about a recovery, or the juice of turnips poured into the nose and mouth. Move the patient into some place where the wind can blow upon him; he may thus come round.

Food
Where poison of some unknown kind has been taken with the food or drink, administer some sweet-grass or *Platycodon grandiflorum* broth; a cure may thus be effected.

CHAPTER THREE
To Cure Cases of Poison by Ku and Chin Ts'an

A Buddhist priest in Chüan-chow could cure cases of *Ku* and *Chin ts'an*. Let the patient begin by tasting alum; if it does not seem astringent, but on the other hand rather sweet, and if black bean taken afterwards has lost its ordinary flavour, then poison has been taken. Administer as a draught a decoction of pomegranate skin and root. If the insect is excreted or thrown up, recovery is certain. Li Hui-chih says: Where poison has been taken, pound up alum and young tea-sprouts, and drink with cold water.

Prescription:

Potato half an ounce; Orpiment, half ounce; Cinnabar, 1 ounce (pounded fine); Yellow oxide of lead (Massicot); Musk; Cantharides, 2and a half mace, with the heads and feet taken off.; Glutinous rice, half raw, half cooked; Red centipedes, one live, one roasted; Croton seeds from Szech'uan ...

Put the above ingredients into a mortar and mix them up together, either on the 5th of the 5th moon, the 9th of the 9th moon, or the 8th of the 12th moon, in some place quite away from women, fowls and dogs. Make up into pills with glutinous rice water, about the size of lung-an stones, and let them dry in a dark place in an earthenware pot. Swallow a little tea with every one you take, being careful not to chew them. In a little while the poison will be excreted, the pills passing away with the clotted blood. If the pills are then washed and preserved their power will be increased threefold.

For all kinds of *ku* poison take dried eel, powder it and swallow on an empty stomach; or take it when cooked and strong-smelling. Those marked with coloured stripes are the best.

126

Herbert Allen GILES (1845-1935)

Herbert Allen Giles was born in Oxford on 18th December 1845, the fourth son of an Anglican clergyman and Fellow of Corpus Christi College. His father had doctrinal differences with the Church and Giles' agnosticism and anti-clericalism no doubt had their origins in his father's ordeal at the hands of the Church of England.

After four years at Charterhouse, Giles went to Peking, having passed the competitive examination for a Student Interpretership in China. He had time and abundant energy to devote to Chinese research and publication, with the result that when he retired on health grounds, at the age of 47, after 25 years' service, he had established a reputation as a Sinologist which enabled him, despite his lack of formal qualifications, to advance to one of the most prestigious academic posts in Chinese studies.

The Chair of Chinese at Cambridge had been vacant since the death in 1895 of its first incumbent, Sir Thomas Wade. Giles was unanimously elected on 3rd December 1897.

There were no other Sinologists at Cambridge and his students were very few. Giles was free to spend his time amongst the Chinese books presented by Wade, of which he became Honorary Keeper, publishing what he gleaned from his wide reading. He finally retired in 1932 and died, in his ninetieth year, on 13th February 1935.

Of all his publications he was most proud of his *Chinese-English Dictionary* (1892; 2nd ed. 1912) and *Chinese Biographical Dictionary* (1898). Today the *Dictionary* is most often cited as the *locus classicus* of the so-called "Wade-Giles" romanisation system, for which the name of Giles is widely known even to non-specialists. Paradoxically, it is his miscellaneous and "ephemeral" writing which now seems most likely to have permanent value and interest. An example is

Chinese Sketches (1876), containing observations based on nine years' residence in China on such varied topics as dentistry, etiquette, gambling, pawnbrokers, slang, superstitions and torture.

As a polemicist, Giles expressed particularly strong views on female infanticide in China, opium addiction which he deemed preferable to alcoholism, and missionary work in China, which he considered undesirable and unnecessary.

Giles was a complex and contradictory personality. He was the soul of kindness to a friend in need. An ardent agnostic, he was at the same time an enthusiastic freemason. He was by all accounts a convivial companion and clubman, and was remembered by acquaintances as a man of great personal charm.

Abridged from:
East Asian History (1997)
Charles Aylmer

Made in the USA
Lexington, KY
11 October 2014